CAROL HIGGINS CLARK, a writer and actress, is the daughter of Mary Higgins Clark. Her highly acclaimed Regan Reilly mysteries include the *New York Times* best-sellers *Twanged, Snagged, Iced,* and *Decked,* which was nominated for both the Agatha and Anthony Awards for Best First Novel.

NELSON DeMILLE, a member of the Mystery Writers of America, began writing novels of the NYPD in 1973. His first major novel was *By the Rivers of Babylon,* followed by *Cathedral, The Talbot Odyssey, Word of Honor, The Charm School, The Gold Coast, The General's Daughter, Spencerville* and *Plum Island.* This is his first collaboration with his daughter.

LAUREN DeMILLE is currently a student at Columbia University. Born and raised on Long Island, New York, she was editor-in-chief of her high school newspaper, and a contributor to the yearbook and to school publications, including the literary magazine. This is her first short-story collaboration.

JANET EVANOVICH is the national best-selling author of the Stephanie Plum novels *One for the Money, Two for the Dough* and *Three to Get Deadly.* Winner of the Creasey and Dilys awards, she lives in New Hampshire, where she is at work on her next novel.

LINDA FAIRSTEIN, America's foremost prosecutor of crimes of sexual assault, has run the Sex Crimes Unit of the District Attorney's Office in Manhattan for more than two decades. She is the author of a nonfiction book, *Sexual Violence,* and two crime novels in the Alexandra Cooper series, *Likely to Die* and *Final Jeopardy.* She lives in Manhattan.

It's no mystery where to find today's best-loved and best-selling mystery and crime writers . . . they're all here in THE PLOT THICKENS!

These contributors have donated their talent and time to fight illiteracy—which affects more than ninety million Americans—through Literacy Partners, a not-for-profit organization that teaches reading through local and national programs.

LAWRENCE BLOCK's crime fiction ranges from the urban noir of Matthew Scudder *(Even the Wicked)* to the urbane effervescence of Bernie Rhodenbarr *(The Burglar in the Library).* A multiple winner of the Edgar and Shamus Awards, he has been named a Grand Master by the Mystery Writers of America.

EDNA BUCHANAN won the Pulitzer Prize in 1986 for her crime reporting. She is the author of three works of nonfiction and eight novels, the latest of which are *Margin of Error* and *Heartbeat.*

MARY HIGGINS CLARK is the best-selling author of sixteen novels, including her latest, *Pretend You Don't See Her,* and three collections of short stories. Born and raised in New York City, she has served as president of Mystery Writers of America. She makes her home in Saddle River, New Jersey.

WALTER MOSLEY, *New York Times* best-selling author of the Easy Rawlins mysteries, is a former president of the Mystery Writers of America. His latest release, *Always Outnumbered, Always Outgunned,* kicks off a new series.

NANCY PICKARD's Jenny Cain mysteries include *Twilight, Confession, Say No to Murder* (Anthony Award–winner), *Marriage Is Murder* (Macavity Award–winner), *Bum Steer* and *I.O.U.* (winners of the Agatha Award for Best Novel). A former reporter and editor, she is a past president of Sisters in Crime, the international association of mystery writers and fans. She lives in Kansas, where she is working on a new mystery to be published by Pocket Books.

ANN RULE, a former Seattle policewoman, is the author of ten *New York Times* true-crime bestsellers, including *The Stranger Beside Me, Dead by Sunset,* and *A Fever in the Heart;* and one *New York Times* best-selling novel, *Possession* (available from Pocket Books). Her newest books, coming in January 1998, are *Bitter Harvest* (Simon & Schuster), and *In the Name of Love* (Pocket Books).

DONALD E. WESTLAKE's newest book is *The Ax.* He has written more than seventy works of fiction, including the classic caper *The Hot Rock.* In 1993, he was named a Grand Master by the Mystery Writers of America. He has won multiple Edgar Awards and received an Oscar nomination for his screenplay of the film *The Grifters.*

MARY HIGGINS CLARK PRESENTS

THE PLOT
Thickens

POCKET BOOKS
New York   London   Toronto   Sydney   Tokyo   Singapore

This book is a work of fiction. Names, characters, places and incidents are products of the authors' imaginations or are used fictitiously. Any resemblance to actual events or locales or persons living or dead is entirely coincidental.

An *Original* Publication of POCKET BOOKS

POCKET BOOKS, a division of Simon & Schuster Inc.
1230 Avenue of the Americas, New York, NY 10020

Copyright © 1997 by Pocket Books

ISBN: 1-56865-526-6

First Pocket Books printing November 1997

POCKET and colophon are registered trademarks of Simon & Schuster Inc.

Cover art by Rick Lovell

Printed in the U.S.A.

Copyright Notices

Contents

ix

CONTENTS

Introduction by Liz Smith

How fortunate you are to be able to read and enjoy this entertaining book! Do you know that forty million adults in this country can't read well enough to do so?

The Plot Thickens came about because Mary Higgins Clark decided to do something about illiteracy in America. She asked ten of her fellow mystery writers to donate a story for this collection, and wrote one herself. Each writer could write anything they wished—and you will see that there is a wide variety of stories—but each story had to contain three items: a thick fog, a thick steak, and a thick book. Besides enjoying the stories themselves, I think you will be amused at the ingenious ways in which each writer worked these three elements into their tales.

All the profits from the sale of this book will go to Literacy Partners, an established and respected nonprofit organization which has, for the last two decades, trained and supervised volunteer tutors to provide free instruction in reading and writing to the hardest-to-serve adult population: those English-speaking men and women who read below the fifth grade level. Recognized as a leader in adult basic education at the local level, Literacy Partners has recently enlarged its mission to be an effective literacy advocate on the national level. Today, it has created and manages a partnership of sixteen exemplary literacy programs throughout the U.S. The goal of this network is to provide its members with the resources to define and document their most effective teaching practices, and to disseminate this information among other literacy programs.

I am proud of the work we have done in the past, and enthusiastic about our plans for the future. We are grateful to Simon & Schuster for publishing this volume on a nonprofit basis, and to Jack Romanos, Gina Centrello, Julie Rubenstein, and Leslie Stern of that company, for all their work in making this book possible.

Liz Smith
Chair, Literacy Partners, Inc.

For more information about Literacy Partners and its programs, please write or phone:

Literacy Partners, Inc.
30 East 33rd Street
New York, N.Y. 10016

Phone: (212) 725-9200
Fax: (212) 725-0414

How Far It Could Go

Lawrence Block

S he picked him out right away, the minute she walked into the restaurant. It was no great trick. There were only two men seated alone, and one was an elderly gentleman who already had a plate of food in front of him.

The other was thirty-five or forty, with a full head of dark hair and a strong jawline. He might have been an actor, she thought. An actor you'd cast as a thug. He was reading a book, though, which didn't entirely fit the picture.

Maybe it wasn't him, she thought. Maybe the weather had delayed him.

She checked her coat, then told the headwaiter she was meeting a Mr. Cutler. "Right this way," he said, and for an instant she fancied that he was going to show her to the elderly gentleman's table, but of course he led her over to the other man, who closed his book at her approach and got to his feet.

"Billy Cutler," he said. "And you're Dorothy Morgan. And you could probably use a drink. What would you like?"

"I don't know," she said. "What are you having?"

"Well," he said, touching his stemmed glass, "night like this, minute I sat down I ordered a martini, straight up and dry as a bone. And I'm about ready for another."

"Martinis are in, aren't they?"

"Far as I'm concerned, they were never out."

"I'll have one," she said.

While they waited for the drinks they talked about the weather. "It's treacherous out there," he said. "The main roads, the Jersey Turnpike and the Garden State, they get these chain collisions where fifty or a hundred cars slam into each other. Used to be a lawyer's dream before no-fault came in. I hope you didn't drive."

"No, I took the PATH train," she said, "and then a cab."

"Much better off."

"Well, I've been to Hoboken before," she said. "In fact we looked at houses here about a year and a half ago."

"You bought anything then, you'd be way ahead now," he said. "Prices are through the roof."

"We decided to stay in Manhattan." And then we decided to go our separate ways, she thought but didn't say. And thank God we didn't buy a house, or he'd be trying to steal it from me.

"I drove," he said, "and the fog's terrible, no question, but I took my time and I didn't have any trouble. Matter of fact, I couldn't remember if we said seven or seven-thirty, so I made sure I was here by seven."

4

"Then I kept you waiting," she said. "I wrote down seven-thirty, but—"

"I figured it was probably seven-thirty," he said. "I also figured I'd rather do the waiting myself than keep you waiting. Anyway"—he tapped the book—"I had a book to read, and I ordered a drink, and what more does a man need? Ah, here's Joe with our drinks."

Her martini, straight up and bone dry, was crisp and cold and just what she needed. She took a sip and said as much.

"Well, there's nothing like a martini," he said, "and they make a good one here. Matter of fact, it's a good restaurant altogether. They serve a good steak, a strip sirloin."

"Also coming back in style," she said. "Along with the martini."

He looked at her. He said, "So? You want to be right up with the latest trends? Should I order us a couple of steaks?"

"Oh, I don't think so," she said. "I really shouldn't stay that long."

"Whatever you say."

"I just thought we'd have a drink and—"

"And handle what we have to handle."

"That's right."

"Sure," he said. "That'll be fine."

Except it was hard to find a way into the topic that had brought her to Hoboken, to this restaurant, to this man's table. They both knew why she was here, but that didn't relieve her of the need to broach the subject. Looking for a way in, she went back to the weather, the fog. Even if the weather had been good, she told him, she would have come by train and taxi. Because she didn't have a car.

He said, "No car? Didn't Tommy say you had a

weekend place up near him? You can't go back and forth on the bus."

"It's his car," she said.

"His car. Oh, the fella's."

"Howard Bellamy's," she said. Why not say his name? "His car, his weekend place in the country. His loft on Greene Street, as far as that goes."

He nodded, his expression thoughtful. "But you're not still living there," he said.

"No, of course not. And I don't have any of my stuff at the house in the country. And I gave back my set of car keys. All my keys, the car and both houses. I kept my old apartment on West Tenth Street all this time. I didn't even sublet it because I figured I might need it in a hurry. And I was right, wasn't I?"

"What's your beef with him exactly, if you don't mind me asking?"

"My beef," she said. "I never had one, far as I was concerned. We lived together three years, and the first two weren't too bad. Trust me, it was never Romeo and Juliet, but it was all right. And then the third year was bad, and it was time to bail out."

She reached for her drink and found the glass empty. Odd—she didn't remember finishing it. She looked across the table at him and he was waiting patiently, nothing showing in his dark eyes.

After a moment she said, "He says I owe him ten thousand dollars."

"Ten large."

"He says."

"Do you?"

She shook her head. "But he's got a piece of paper," she said. "A note I signed."

"For ten thousand dollars."

6

"Right."

"Like he loaned you the money."

"Right." She toyed with her empty glass. "But he didn't. Oh, he's got the paper I signed, and he's got a canceled check made out to me and deposited to my account. But it wasn't a loan. He gave me the money and I used it to pay for a cruise the two of us took."

"Where? The Caribbean?"

"The Far East. We flew into Singapore and cruised down to Bali."

"That sounds pretty exotic."

"I guess it was," she said. "This was while things were still good between us, or as good as they ever were."

"This paper you signed," he prompted.

"Something with taxes. So he could write it off, don't ask me how. Look, all the time we lived together I paid my own way. We split expenses right down the middle. The cruise was something else, it was on him. If he wanted me to sign a piece of paper so the government would pick up part of the tab—"

"Why not?"

"Exactly. And now he says it's a debt, and I should pay it, and I got a letter from his lawyer. Can you believe it? A letter from a lawyer?"

"He's not going to sue you."

"Who knows? That's what the lawyer letter says he's going to do."

He frowned. "He goes into court and you start testifying about a tax dodge—"

"But how can I, if I was a party to it?"

"Still, the idea of him suing you after you were living with him. Usually it's the other way around, isn't it? They got a word for it."

"Palimony."

"That's it, palimony. You're not trying for any, are you?"

"Are you kidding? I said I paid my own way."

"That's right, you said that."

"I paid my own way before I met him, the son of a bitch, and I paid my own way while I was with him, and I'll go on paying my own way now that I'm rid of him. The last time I took money from a man was when my uncle Ralph lent me bus fare to New York when I was eighteen years old. He didn't call it a loan, and he sure as hell didn't give me a piece of paper to sign, but I paid him back all the same. I saved up the money and sent him a money order. I didn't even have a bank account. I got a money order at the post office and sent it to him."

"That's when you came here? When you were eighteen?"

"Fresh out of high school," she said. "And I've been on my own ever since, and paying my own way. I would have paid my own way to Singapore, as far as that goes, but that wasn't the deal. It was supposed to be a present. And he wants me to pay my way and his way, he wants the whole ten thousand plus interest, and—"

"He's looking to charge you interest?"

"Well, the note I signed. Ten thousand dollars plus interest at the rate of eight percent per annum."

"Interest," he said.

"He's pissed off," she said, "that I wanted to end the relationship. That's what this is about."

"I figured."

"And what I figured," she said, "is if a couple of the right sort of people had a talk with him, maybe he would change his mind."

"And that's what brings you here."

She nodded, toying with her empty glass. He pointed to the glass, raised his eyebrows questioningly. She nodded again, and he raised a hand, and caught the waiter's eye, and signaled for another round.

They were silent until the drinks came. Then he said, "A couple of boys could talk to him."

"That would be great. What would it cost me?"

"Five hundred dollars would do it."

"Well, that sounds good to me."

"The thing is, when you say talk, it'll have to be more than talk. You want to make an impression, situation like this, the implication is either he goes along with it or something physical is going to happen. Now, if you want to give that impression, you have to get physical at the beginning."

"So he knows you mean it?"

"So he's scared," he said. "Because otherwise what he gets is angry. Not right away, two tough-looking guys push him against a wall and tell him what he's gotta do. That makes him a little scared right away, but then they don't get physical and he goes home, and he starts to think about it, and he gets angry."

"I can see how that might happen."

"But if he gets knocked around a little the first time, enough so he's gonna feel it for the next four, five days, he's too scared to get angry. That's what you want."

"Okay."

He sipped his drink, looked at her over the brim. His eyes were appraising her, assessing her. "There's things I need to know about the guy."

"Like?"

"Like what kind of shape is he in?"

"He could stand to lose twenty pounds, but other than that he's okay."

"No heart condition, nothing like that?"

"No."

"He work out?"

"He belongs to a gym," she said, "and he went four times a week for the first month after he joined, and now if he goes twice a month it's a lot."

"Like everybody," he said. "That's how the gyms stay in business. If all their paid-up members showed up, you couldn't get in the door."

"You work out," she said.

"Well, yeah," he said. "Weights, mostly, a few times a week. I got in the habit. I won't tell you where I got in the habit."

"And I won't ask," she said, "but I could probably guess."

"You probably could," he said, grinning. He looked like a little boy for an instant, and then the grin faded and he was back to business.

"Martial arts," he said. "He ever get into any of that?"

"No."

"You're sure? Not lately, but maybe before the two of you started keeping company?"

"He never said anything," she said, "and he would. It's the kind of thing he'd brag about."

"Does he carry?"

"Carry?"

"A gun."

"God, no."

"You know this for a fact?"

"He doesn't even own a gun."

"Same question. Do you know this for a fact?"

10

She considered it. "Well, how would you know something like that for a fact? I mean, you could know for a fact that a person *did* own a gun, but how would you know that he didn't? I can say this much— I lived with him for three years and there was never anything I saw or heard that gave me the slightest reason to think he might own a gun. Until you asked the question just now it never entered my mind, and my guess is it never entered *his* mind, either."

"You'd be surprised how many people own guns," he said.

"I probably would."

"Sometimes it feels like half the country walks around strapped. There's more carrying than there are carry permits. A guy doesn't have a permit, he's likely to keep it to himself that he's carrying, or that he even owns a gun in the first place."

"I'm pretty sure he doesn't own a gun, let alone carry one."

"And you're probably right," he said, "but the thing is you never know. What you got to prepare for is he *might* have a gun, and he *might* be carrying it."

She nodded, uncertain.

"Here's what I've got to ask you," he said. "What you got to ask yourself, and come up with an answer. How far are you prepared for this to go?"

"I'm not sure what you mean."

"We already said it's gonna be physical. Manhandling him, and a couple of shots he'll feel for the better part of a week. Work the rib cage, say."

"All right."

"Well," he said, "that's great, if that's how it goes. But you got to recognize it could go farther."

"What do you mean?"

He made a tent of his fingertips. "I mean you can't necessarily decide where it stops. I don't know if you ever heard the expression, but it's like, uh, having relations with a gorilla. You don't stop when you decide. You stop when the gorilla decides."

"I never heard that before," she said. "It's cute, and I sort of get the point, or maybe I don't. Is Howard Bellamy the gorilla?"

"He's not the gorilla. The violence is the gorilla."

"Oh."

"You start something, you don't know where it goes. Does he fight back? If he does, then it goes a little farther than you planned. Does he keep coming back for more? As long as he keeps coming back for it, you got to keep dishing it out. You got no choice."

"I see."

"Plus there's the human factor. The boys themselves, they don't have an emotional stake. So you figure they're cool and professional about it."

"That's what I figured."

"But it's only true up to a point," he went on, "because they're human, you know? So they start out angry with the guy, they tell themselves how he's a low-life piece of garbage, so it's easier for them to shove him around. Part of it's an act but part of it's not, and say he mouths off, or he fights back and gets in a good lick. Now they're really angry, and maybe they do more damage than they intended to."

She thought about it. "I can see how that could happen," she said.

"So it could go farther than anybody had in mind. He could wind up in the hospital."

"You mean like broken bones?"

"Or worse. Like a ruptured spleen, which I've known of cases. Or as far as that goes there's people

12

who've died from a bare-knuckle punch in the stomach."

"I saw a movie where that happened."

"Well, I saw a movie where a guy spreads his arms and flies, but dying from a punch in the stomach, they didn't just make that up for the movies. It can happen."

"Now you've got me thinking," she said.

"Well, it's something you got to think about. Because you have to be prepared for this to go all the way, and by all the way I mean all the way. It probably won't, ninety-five times out of a hundred it won't."

"But it could."

"Right. It could."

"Jesus," she said. "He's a son of a bitch, but I don't want him dead. I want to be done with the son of a bitch. I don't want him on my conscience for the rest of my life."

"That's what I figured."

"But I don't want to pay him ten thousand dollars, either, the son of a bitch. This is getting complicated, isn't it?"

"Let me excuse myself for a minute," he said, rising. "And you think about it, and then we'll talk some more."

While he was away from the table she reached for his book and turned it so she could read the title. She looked at the author's photo, read a few lines of the flap copy, then put it as he had left it. She sipped her drink—she was nursing this one, making it last—and looked out the window. Cars rolled by, their headlights slightly eerie in the dense fog.

When he returned she said, "Well, I thought about it."

"And?"

"I think you just talked yourself out of five hundred dollars."

"That's what I figured."

"Because I certainly don't want him dead, and I don't even want him in the hospital. I have to admit I like the idea of him being scared, really scared bad. And hurt a little. But that's just because I'm angry."

"Anybody'd be angry."

"But when I get past the anger," she said, "all I really want is for him to forget this crap about ten thousand dollars. For Christ's sake, that's all the money I've got in the world. I don't want to give it to him."

"Maybe you don't have to."

"What do you mean?"

"I don't think it's about money," he said. "Not for him. It's about sticking it to you for dumping him, or whatever. So it's an emotional thing and it's easy for you to buy into it. But say it was a business thing. You're right and he's wrong, but it's more trouble than it's worth to fight it out. So you settle."

"Settle?"

"You always paid your own way," he said, "so it wouldn't be out of the question for you to pay half the cost of the cruise, would it?"

"No, but—"

"But it was supposed to be a present, from him to you. But forget that for the time being. You could pay half. Still, that's too much. What you do is you offer him two thousand dollars. I have a feeling he'll take it."

"God," she said. "I can't even talk to him. How am I going to offer him anything?"

"You'll have someone else make the offer."

"You mean like a lawyer?"

"Then you owe the lawyer. No, I was thinking I could do it."

"Are you serious?"

"I wouldn't have said it if I wasn't. I think if I was to make the offer he'd accept it. I wouldn't be threatening him, but there's a way to do it so a guy feels threatened."

"He'd feel threatened, all right."

"I'll have your check with me, two thousand dollars, payable to him. My guess is he'll take it, and if he does you won't hear any more from him on the subject of the ten grand."

"So I'm out of it for two thousand. And five hundred for you?"

"I wouldn't charge you anything."

"Why not?"

"All I'd be doing is having a conversation with a guy. I don't charge for conversations. I'm not a lawyer, I'm just a guy owns a couple of parking lots."

"And reads thick novels by young Indian writers."

"Oh, this? You read it?"

She shook her head.

"It's hard to keep the names straight," he said, "especially when you're not sure how to pronounce them in the first place. And it's like if you ask this guy what time it is he tells you how to make a watch. Or maybe a sundial. But it's pretty interesting."

"I never thought you'd be a reader."

"Billy Parking Lots," he said. "Guy who knows guys and can get things done. That's probably all Tommy said about me."

"Just about."

"Maybe that's all I am. Reading, well, it's an edge I got on just about everybody I know. It opens other worlds. I don't live in those worlds, but I get to visit them."

"And you just got in the habit of reading? The way you got in the habit of working out?"

He laughed. "Yeah, but reading's something I've done since I was a kid. I didn't have to go away to get in that particular habit."

"I was wondering about that."

"Anyway," he said, "it's hard to read there, harder than people think. It's noisy all the time."

"Really? I didn't realize. I always figured that's when I'd get to read *War and Peace,* when I got sent to prison. But if it's noisy, then the hell with it. I'm not going."

"You're something else," he said.

"Me?"

"Yeah, you. The way you look, of course, but beyond the looks. The only word I can think of is *class,* but it's a word that's mostly used by people that haven't got any themselves. Which is probably true enough."

"The hell with that," she said. "After the conversation we just had? Talking me out of doing something I could have regretted all my life, *and* figuring out how to get that son of a bitch off my back for two thousand dollars? I'd call that class."

"Well, you're seeing me at my best," he said.

"And you're seeing me at my worst," she said, "or close to it. Looking to hire a guy to beat up an ex-boyfriend. That's class, all right."

"That's not what I see. I see a woman who doesn't want to be pushed around. And if I can find a way that helps you get where you want to be, then I'm glad to

16

do it. But when all's said and done, you're a lady and I'm a wiseguy."

"I don't know what you mean."

"Yes, you do."

"Yes, I guess I do."

He nodded. "Drink up," he said. "I'll run you back to the city."

"You don't have to do that. I can take the PATH train."

"I've got to go into the city anyway. It's not out of my way to take you wherever you're going."

"If you're sure."

"I'm sure," he said. "Or here's another idea. We both have to eat, and I told you they serve a good steak here. Let me buy you dinner, and *then* I'll run you home."

"Dinner," she said.

"A shrimp cocktail, a salad, a steak, a baked potato—"

"You're tempting me."

"So let yourself be tempted," he said. "It's just a meal."

She looked at him levelly. "No," she said. "It's more than that."

"It's more than that if you want it to be. Or it's just a meal, if that's what you want."

"But you can't know how far it might go," she said. "We're back to that again, aren't we? Like what you said about the gorilla, and you stop when the gorilla wants to stop."

"I guess I'm the gorilla, huh?"

"You said the violence was the gorilla. Well, in this case it's not violence, but it's not either of us, either. It's what's going on between us, and it's already going on, isn't it?"

17

"You tell me."

She looked down at her hands, then up at him. "A person has to eat," she said.

"You said it."

"And it's still foggy outside."

"Like pea soup. And who knows? There's a good chance the fog'll lift by the time we've had our meal."

"I wouldn't be a bit surprised," she said. "I think it's lifting already."

Foolproof

Edna Buchanan

N aked, on a metal tray at the morgue, Junior Wallace still wore the arrogant grin cops hated, but now it exposed badly broken front teeth. Somebody had tattooed his chest with a trio of slugs as he stood at the top of a staircase. His teeth had broken during the fall. A plastic tube inserted by an overeager paramedic protruded from his left nostril, the loose end flung jauntily over his shoulder like some new fashion accessory.

Nobody would cry for Wallace, Detective Dan Flood thought as he watched the autopsy. The man died like he lived. This was one of those moments Flood appreciated, live long enough and sometimes you see justice. Rarely had he seen it provided by the system, always exacted instead by time, fate or some higher power.

Junior Wallace had been a chronic irritant during much of Dan's twenty-five years of police work. Twice during his long career as a homicide detective he had nailed Junior for murder. Twice the system had let him walk. The first time, a savvy defense attorney outclassed a novice prosecutor with a legal technicality. The second time, all charges were dismissed after they lost the eyewitnesses, one dead, the other too frightened to testify.

Dan knew Junior to be the shooter in three other cases he could never prove. He and his brothers had run Miami cops ragged, accumulating rap sheets as long as they were tall. One brother was serving twenty-five years mandatory minimum for murder, the other was taking the big dirt sleep in potter's field.

"Glad he's finally out of circulation," Flood said. "He was overdue. This guy thought defensive driving meant wearing a bulletproof vest."

"Well, he didn't wear one when it counted," said Dr. George Webb, the Dade County Medical Examiner conducting the autopsy.

Webb was drawing a urine specimen, filling a syringe.

"He'll test positive for something," Flood predicted. "These guys never change. Had to be something genetic—entire family was a walking crime wave."

"What was your relationship with my victim?" The young homicide detective's possessive tone made it clear that this was her case.

"Relationship?" he said mildly. "Same as the one between the sole of my shoe and a palmetto bug. Any idea who did him?"

"We've got some leads." He waited, but she did not elaborate.

Flood was solving murders when she was still being burped on somebody's shoulder, but it was apparent she was not about to share what she knew nor ask his professional advice. Steamed, he watched her swagger off. His indignation filled the foul air.

"Forget it," the doctor said, peering up from the canoelike incision between Junior's sternum and his pubic bone. "Let her learn the hard way. Listen," he dropped his voice. "Six o'clock tomorrow afternoon. Be here."

"What for?"

"You've never seen an autopsy like the one we're planning." His round pink face shone with promise, his eyes shielding a secret.

"I thought nothing came through here that I haven't seen before." Curiosity prickled, a sensation he had not felt for a long time.

"What is it, an animal?" Flood knew the medical examiner had conducted necropsies when Jimmy, the giant gorilla, suffered a fatal heart attack at Metro Zoo, and on a goat, in a fruitless attempt to quell rumors among Miami's superstitious Spanish speaking community that the *chupacabra,* a mythical vampire blood sucker, was stalking pets and farm animals.

"Nope, this is an old case." Webb refused to divulge more.

The following afternoon Flood arrived early, the limp from his old gunshot wound always more pronounced by day's end. He entered the fortresslike building through the loading dock, past the old railroad scale still used to weigh incoming corpses, and the counter where morgue attendants bar coded bodies like supermarket products to avoid unfortunate mix-ups.

The younger attendants ignored him but the veterans still greeted him by name. "How you doing, Dan?" asked one old-timer.

"Still vertical," he said.

"How's the new job?"

"So boring that I'd sooner have root canal." Working with computer technology was a yawn after all the years on the street matching wits with murder suspects. Was he the only man in the world, he wondered, who felt nostalgia for the morgue? What did that say about his private life, what little there was. He had lived alone since his marriage became a casualty of the job a dozen years ago. His children were grown and scattered. Homicide had been his family and his home.

He and Dr. Webb had weathered the invasions of cocaine cowboys, Marieletos and Haitian boat people. They had tracked serial killers and mob hit men, and sorted through the carnage left by deadly hurricanes, disastrous plane crashes and tragic building collapses. Now Flood languished in the ID unit adjacent to the crime lab, matching wits only with shiny machines, high-tech computers and microscopes.

When he was first transferred out of homicide, the young hotshot detectives and cold case squad investigators frequently sought him out when they needed advice, or when new information came to light on one of his old cases. But those calls came less often now.

Though Hood was early, his secretary said Dr. Webb was already down in the pit, the autopsy room. When the detective entered, he saw that this postmortem was being conducted in privacy, away from the crowded surgical suite. The doctor and several strangers had already suited up. An ID tech from the morgue and two photographers stood by, one with a video camera on his shoulder.

"Glad you made it." Webb handed him a mask and a gown. "This is one for your memoirs."

Flood gaped at the body on the table. When the medical examiner said old case, he meant an *old* case.

"Jesus," he said. "I never seen one of these before. Closest I ever had to this was that little kid wrapped in sheets and newspapers and walled up in a closet for four, five years."

"Yes," Webb said, "I remember that case. This gentleman is older, by a few thousand years." He introduced the other observers, who had foreign-sounding names, and then the guest of honor.

"This fellow was on tour with the exhibit of ancient artifacts from the Cairo Museum when they noticed something wrong. He was deteriorating fast, some sort of fungus, probably due to changes in atmosphere and climate, so the people in charge"—he nodded at the strangers—"elected to do a postmortem here, rather than lose the opportunity forever."

Speaking into the overhead mike, Webb said, "From what I understand, the objects and hieroglyphics found with the mummy indicate that this gentleman was a feudal lord, a bit of a troublemaker, with connections to the royal family—well known in his time, perhaps even notorious. According to the Egyptologists who made those determinations, all evidence and the markings found with him indicate that death occurred in approximately 1102 B.C. due to natural causes."

The mummy, Webb noted, was that of a man in his thirties. Forensics had already begun work on his hands. They had been removed, the fingers severed and placed in ten individually labeled vials, which rested now in a small rack on a nearby table. Otherwise, the mummy appeared intact.

The cameramen hovered, recording the proceedings as Webb delicately removed the rest of the wrappings. A gumlike resinous substance adhered to the ancient linen as it fell away. Bright overhead lights exposed crusty white blotches on the shriveled leather of the dead man's skin. "Appears to be some sort of salt," Webb observed, "perhaps used in the embalming process. Ancient Egyptians believed in the resurrection of a spiritual body and the immortality of the soul," he said, as he looked up. "They believed in life beyond the grave."

What would the dead man think, Flood wondered, if he awoke from his endless slumber and saw where his long voyage from antiquity had brought him? How would he react to the soulless eye of an Insta cam?

The mummy's eyes were covered with folds of woven fabric impregnated with resin. Webb removed them with tweezers. The nostrils were packed with similar material.

"It would be fascinating," Webb said, "if we could actually determine what this fellow died of. But the absence of internal organs makes that highly unlikely."

"Looks like a prizefighter, a two-bit pug," Flood said.

Webb nodded. "The nose cartilage is flattened, probably by the pressure of the bandages." The skin was grayish, cracked and brittle.

"Let's take his fingerprints now." The doctor nodded to the technician.

"No way you can print this guy," Flood said.

"Nonsense." Webb stepped back to allow the ID tech room to work. "We print every body that comes in here."

26

Flood lifted a skeptical eyebrow. It was one thing to work on decomposed corpses, especially those found submerged, as was so often the case in Miami. Saturated skin separates. The epidermis, the outer layer, often slips off, as smoothly as a glove. Wearing that skin over his gloved fingers, a technician can roll the fingerprints as though they were his own. Flood had seen it done many times. But mummified bodies were something else.

The technician, a small, intense man, specialized in working on unidentified corpses. "We've had some success with a recently discovered mummified body," he explained. "We were able to flatten skin from the fingers between glass, photograph it and get enough ridge detail for prints.

"But we're trying something totally different here," he went on, "something devised by a technician in the Wisconsin State crime lab." He looked pleased. "As you can see, we've been soaking the fingers in an embalming solution called Permaflow.

"As they soaked, a white mold began to spread over the fingers. After we wiped it away and kept soaking, the skin and tissues softened, regained their color and almost appear to be living tissue."

"Yeah." Flood peered closely at one of the vials the technician had opened. "And there's no smell."

"That's right," the tech said, "no putrefication, no decomposition."

One by one, he pressed the fingertips flat to remove wrinkles and dusted them with black fingerprint powder. Then he pressed each ancient digit onto Kinderprint Poly Tape.

"I'm impressed," Flood said. The mummy's gaping grin was making him uncomfortable, reminding him in some otherworldly way of the smirk worn by the recently deceased Junior Wallace. It said "bad to the bone."

Dr. Webb carefully unwound a coarse yellowed cloth from around the dead man's legs and feet. The shock came when he and an attendant turned the body.

"Well," the doctor said, amid startled murmurs from the others. "What have we here?"

The back of the dead Egyptian's skull had been caved in by a weapon that left a distinct indentation.

"Whadaya know?" Flood said. "Looks like somebody took an ax to the back of his head."

"If we had the weapon we could probably match it to the wound," the doctor said. "I would say it was definitely a hatchet or an ax." He looked hopefully at the men from the museum who shook their heads, expressing astonishment.

X rays also revealed a fractured ulna, a typical defense wound to the forearm.

"Well, gentlemen," Webb concluded, "looks like we've got a homicide."

"A whodunit," Flood said gleefully. "A cover-up. They lied when they said natural causes did this guy. Told ya." He nudged the doctor. "People never change. Hadda be an inside job. The ones who did the embalming musta known. Lies, intrigue and cover-ups. Who the hell knows what kinda politics and power plays were going on back then?"

"Probably not so different than those that go on around us today," Webb said. "These ancients weren't so different from us in many ways. The Egyptians were beer drinkers for one thing. Had a king named Pepi. There was a Pepi the First and Pepi the Second, if I recall correctly." He turned to the museum experts.

They agreed.

"And one had a royal relative named Sheri."

"Sheri and Pepi." Flood chortled. "Sounds like a stripper and a hustler I usta know."

The men from the museum were not amused.

"Another unsolved case," Webb said. "I thought it was tough inheriting those delayed World War Two fatalities."

"Yeah," Flood explained to the others. "A lotta World War Two vets retired to Miami. Every once in a while one dies of seizures or complications related to old war wounds. I had a case, just before I transferred, guy died at the VFW post. The doc, here, had to list 'gunshot wound' as the cause of death. Drives up the numbers on unsolved homicides. Who's gonna try to track down the killer, some enemy soldier who fired a gun on Bataan or Corregidor back then? If the shooter survived the war, he's either long dead or a successful car manufacturer."

The hour was late by the time they finished.

"A souvenir," Webb said, on the way out. He gave Flood a copy of the mummy's fingerprint card.

The prints looked perfect. The new technique worked well. Flood slipped the card into his briefcase, snapped it shut and grinned. "You were right, Doc," he said. "This was one for the books."

The fascinating events that unfolded that evening sustained him through the tedious day that followed, teaching a recent police academy graduate the intricacies of AFIS. The Automatic Fingerprint Identification System had been recently linked to the national database. Prints fed into the computer were compared at eleven thousand per second with those in county records. If no match was found, the search automatically proceeded to nearly two million sets of prints in the statewide data base, then on to Washington, D.C., for a nationwide search.

The new recruit wore frizzy blond hair and too much makeup. She had attended the police academy as part of a government rehabilitation program aimed at moving welfare mothers off public assistance and onto a payroll.

Justice, that rare commodity, would now rest at times, Flood thought grimly, in the hands of this woman who demonstrated the IQ of Spam.

"Take this." He plopped a big, thick book onto her lap. *The Science of Criminal Investigation,* eight hundred and forty-three pages. "Read the section on fingerprints tonight. That's your homework."

Her eyes widened, her mouth opened into a perfect little circle. "I'm gonna ask questions," he warned.

She opened the book, frowning at the first page as she twisted a lock of hair between blood-red acrylic fingernails, then squinted up at him. "Do they pay me overtime for reading this at home?"

He took a deep breath. "Here," he said impatiently. "Lemme see how you run a fingerprint search."

"By myself?"

"I've shown you half a dozen times."

He reached into his briefcase and pulled out Mummy Doe's fingerprint card. "See if you can come up with something on this guy."

He watched as she settled in front of the twenty-one-inch AFIS monitor, slipped the card into a glass-enclosed box that resembled a slide viewer and used the keyboard. The prints materialized, larger than life, on the screen. "See." He tried to keep his voice civil. "You can do it. Now scan the prints in standard order—right thumb, index, middle, ring, little, then left thumb. That's it."

Within seconds the high-speed scanner reported NIF, not in file, for the county, and the set of prints was transmitted to the state database. "Looks like you've got it down." He handed her half a dozen other cards. "Run these, too."

Flood was sipping black coffee when she stopped by his desk. It was nearly quitting time and she was poised to be first out the door. "That scan I did," she said, almost as an afterthought. "It came back a hit. Thought you'd like to know."

"A hit? Which one?"

"The first one—the first one I tried."

Oh sheesh, he thought. She screwed it up.

"San Francisco PD. The guy's got a rap sheet a mile long," she said over her shoulder as she headed out. "The info's on my desk."

"Didn't you forget something?"

She blanked, then smacked her forehead and scurried back for the big, thick book. "I could use this for a doorstop," she said bleakly.

The woman could screw up a one-car funeral, Flood thought. "What the hell did she do here?" he wondered aloud, examining the response from Frisco. Mummy Doe's prints had been identified as those of a gang-affiliated career criminal named Desmond Streeter aka Pharaoh. Flood sighed and sat down heavily in front of the screen to see what had gone wrong.

Still in his office dictating a paper, Dr. Webb picked up the ringing phone.

"The tour that mummy was on," Flood asked, "did it stop in San Francisco?"

"No," Webb said. "My understanding was that the

31

exhibit left Paris for New York, came here, and will travel on to Chicago."

"Well, something's funny, Doc. Somebody else musta printed him."

"No way, the mummy was intact, the hands still wrapped before we treated them."

"Well, listen to this. Two print examiners in San Francisco agree that the prints on Mummy Doe's card match all ten of some street punk, a gang member, most recent arrest two weeks ago."

The doctor chuckled. "What did they say when you told them?"

"I didn't. I wanted to check with you first."

"It's impossible, Dan."

"I know. Why d'you think I didn't tell 'em? Something's haywire. Oh, and the punk's street name? Pharaoh. Somebody's jerking our chain."

The two met in the lab an hour later and examined the original prints from the mummy. They matched the set transmitted by AFIS.

"Wouldn't it be something, if . . ."

"Impossible," Dr. Webb said.

Desmond Streeter's prints arrived by FedEx next morning per Flood's request. He mistrusted the accuracy of those transmitted by fax. He walked them over to the medical examiner's building. The prints matched.

They sat in Webb's small office staring at each other.

Flood shook his head. "She puts it in the machine, a routine test, and boom! This happens."

"Nothing happened," the doctor insisted. "Fingerprinting is the only foolproof method of identification. It is superior to DNA. Even identical twins don't have the same prints. They share the same DNA, but never the same fingerprints. I don't even think cloning would produce this. Of all the prints filed all over the world, no print has ever been replicated!"

"Yeah, this would be the first in world history," Flood said.

"It can't happen." Webb shook his head.

The answer, they finally agreed, was to go to San Francisco, find Desmond Streeter, print him themselves and make their own comparison.

They told no one. Neither wanted to be ridiculed. Flood had comp time coming and Webb took vacation days. They said they were going fishing. Flood wished they were. He bitched all the way to the airport.

He could not leave it alone, even on the flight.

"What are the odds?" he asked Webb as the flight attendant served drinks. "If no two prints have ever matched, the odds have to be astronomical."

"The possibility of somebody having the same set of ten are one in a billion—times ten. And that's conservative."

"But what if . . . ?"

The doctor shook his head. "It defies logic."

"But what if . . . ?" he persisted.

"Then it's big." Their eyes caught. "Network nightly news big, *Today Show* big. Big as on the front pages of every newspaper and scientific journal."

"Yeah," Flood said. "So big that the whole criminal justice system would turn into chaos. Imagine what the Johnnie Cochrans of the world would do with it."

Webb nodded. "Every conviction predicated on fingerprint evidence would be appealed. The whole system worldwide would go into crisis." The prospect shocked them into silence for the rest of the long flight.

They fought off the hare krishnas at the airport and rented a car. During the drive into the city they passed what used to be Candlestick Park. "Whadda they call it now?" Flood griped. "Three Com Park? Jeeze, just like they renamed Joe Robbie Stadium. There ain't no justice."

They checked into the hotel, then found a good restaurant. Flood dined heartily on a thick steak while Webb picked at his seafood. They discussed how to talk Streeter into letting them print him. His rap sheet did not indicate a history of cooperation with the authorities.

"Maybe we could buy him a greasy chicken dinner, then steal his glass," Flood suggested.

Desmond Streeter lived in Fillmore, an apartment in a crumbling old Victorian mansion, overlooking the long-shuttered Winterland Ball Room. Flood and Webb had been warned not to cruise the tough neighborhood alone in a rental car at night, but no problem. Emergency vehicles surrounded the building, their revolving lights splashing eerily across the shadows. A patrolman was stringing yellow crime scene tape when they parked.

"Homicide," he said, and referred them to a supervisor.

Somehow Flood knew that the crime scene would be Desmond Streeter's apartment.

A detective emerged. "Looks like Pharaoh finally bought it," he told the patrolman with a grin.

* * *

FOOLPROOF

Desmond Streeter stared at the ceiling from his living room floor, his body an island in a sea of blood.

"Probably gang related," said the Frisco detective. "We have a turf war going on here." He squatted, to scrutinize the body. "Don't see where he's hit."

Dr. Webb and the local medic knew each other from meetings of the National Academy of Forensic Sciences. Both donned rubber gloves. Flood watched.

"Looks like an injury here, some trauma to his arm," the local doctor commented.

Flood's stomach flipped into a free fall.

"Let's . . . turn him over," Dr. Webb suggested.

The back of Streeter's skull was broken and ugly. "Maybe he wasn't shot," said the detective.

"I agree," Webb said. "I'd venture to say that when he's cleaned up, it will prove to be an ax or hatchet wound."

"You may be right," the other doctor said.

They followed the wagon to the morgue. After the dead man was weighed, measured and fingerprinted, Dan Flood rolled a set of prints for himself. He and Webb had explained that they were looking at Streeter for a possible connection to an old homicide case in Miami. No lie there.

"Never knew Pharaoh to travel out of this jurisdiction," the San Francisco detective said, "but it wouldn't surprise me if he took a little vacation. This guy was bad news wherever he was. People don't change."

"No," Flood said, "they don't." He handed the fresh fingerprint card to Dr. Webb, along with the one they had brought with them. Even to the naked eye all ten prints were an obvious match.

* * *

Both men were silent as they left the morgue. Webb drove.

"Hey," Flood said later, startled at what loomed before them. "You're lost. This isn't the way to our hotel. You're on the damn Golden Gate Bridge!"

"Just wanted to see it," Webb said softly. "The most beautiful bridge in the world. I've never understood why they haven't installed a suicide fence. More than twelve hundred people have jumped from this span. It's two hundred and thirty-five feet down." He pulled over and stopped, opened the driver's side door and stepped out into the cold night air. Thick fog surrounded them, billowing beneath the span like clouds beneath a jet plane.

"Ya ain't gonna jump, are ya, Doc?"

"No." Webb reached back into the car for the fingerprint cards of Mummy Doe and Desmond "Pharaoh" Streeter.

The men's eyes locked for a long moment. Then the doctor closed the door and walked to the railing. Flood rolled down his window to watch as Webb tore the cards in half, then in quarters, then leaned over the railing to let the pieces go. Fluttering in the air for a moment, they vanished into the rolling fog that swept in off the dark sea.

The Man Next Door

Mary Higgins Clark

The man next door had known for weeks that it was time to invite another guest to the secret place, the space he had fashioned out of the utility room in the basement. It had been six months since Tiffany, the last one. She had lasted twenty days, longer than most of the others.

He had tried to put Bree Matthews out of his mind. It didn't make sense to invite her, he knew that. Every morning as he followed his routine, washing the windows, polishing the furniture, vacuuming the carpets, sweeping and washing the walk from the steps to the sidewalk, he reminded himself that it was dangerous to choose a next-door neighbor. *Much* too dangerous.

But he couldn't help it. Bree Matthews was never out of his mind for an instant. Ever since the day she had rung his bell and he had invited her in, he had known. That was when his growing need to have her with him became uncontrollable. She had stood in his foyer, dressed in a loose sweater and jeans, her arms folded, one high-arched foot unconsciously tapping the polished floor as she told him that the leak in her adjoining town house was originating from *his* roof.

"When I bought this place I never thought I'd have so much trouble," she had snapped. "The contractor could have redone Buckingham Palace for what I paid him to renovate, but whenever it rains hard, you'd think I lived under Niagara Falls. Anyway, he *insists* that whoever did your work caused the problem."

Her anger had thrilled him. She was beautiful, in a bold, Celtic way, with midnight blue eyes, fair skin, and blue-black hair. And beneath that she had a slim athlete's body. He guessed her to be in her late twenties, older than the women he usually favored, but still so very appealing.

He had known that even though it was a warm spring afternoon, there was no excuse for the way perspiration began to pour from him as he stood a few inches from her. He wanted so much to reach out and touch her, to push the door closed, to lock her in.

He had blushed and stammered as he explained that there was absolutely no possibility that the leak was coming from his roof, that he'd done all the repairs himself. He suggested she call another contractor for an opinion.

He had almost explained that he had worked for a builder for fifteen years and knew that the guy she had hired was doing a shoddy job, but he managed to stop himself. He didn't want to admit that he had any interest in her or her home, didn't want her to know that he had even noticed, didn't want to give anything about himself away . . . .

A few days later she came up the street as he was outside planting impatiens along the driveway, and stopped to apologize. Following his advice, she had called in a different contractor who confirmed what she had suspected: the first one had done a sloppy job. "He'll hear from me in court," she vowed. "I've had a summons issued for him."

Then, emboldened by her friendliness, he did something foolish. As he stood with her, he was facing their semidetached town houses and once again noticed the lopsided venetian blind on her front window, the one nearest his place. Every time he saw it, it drove him crazy. The vertical blinds on his front windows and those on hers lined up perfectly, which made the sight of that lopsided one bother him as much as hearing a fingernail screech across a blackboard.

So he offered to fix it for her. She turned and looked at the offending blind as if she had never seen it before, then she replied, "Thanks, but why bother? The decorator has window treatments ready to put in as soon as the damage caused by the leaks is repaired. It'll get fixed then."

"Then," of course, could be months from now, but still he was glad she had said no. He had definitely decided to invite her to be his next guest, and when she disappeared there would be questions. The police would ring his bell, make inquiries. "Mr. Mensch, did you see Miss Matthews leave with anyone?" they would ask. "Did you notice anyone visiting her lately? How friendly were you with her?"

He could answer truthfully: "We only spoke casually on the street if we ran into each other. She has a young man she seems to be dating. I've exchanged a few words with him from time to time. Tall, brown hair, about thirty or so. Believe he said his name is Carter. Kevin Carter."

The police would probably already know about Carter. When Matthews disappeared they would talk to her close friends first.

He had never even been questioned about Tiffany. There had been no connection between them, no reason for anyone to ask. Occasionally they ran into each other at museums—he had found several of his young women in museums. The third or fourth time they met he made it a point to ask Tiffany her impression of a painting she was looking at.

He had liked her instantly. Beautiful Tiffany, so appealing, so intelligent. She believed that because he claimed to share her enthusiasm for Gustav Klimt, he was a kindred spirit, a man to be trusted. She had been grateful for his offer of a ride back to Georgetown on a rainy day. He had picked her up as she was walking to the Metro.

She had scarcely felt the prick of the needle that knocked her out. She slumped at his feet in the car, and he drove her back to his place. Matthews was just leaving her house as he pulled into the driveway; he even nodded to her as he clicked the garage door opener. At that time he had no idea that Matthews would be next, of course.

Every morning for the next three weeks, he had spent all his time with Tiffany. He loved having her there. The secret place was bright and cheerful. The floor had a thick yellow pad, like a comfortable mattress, and he had filled the room with books and games.

He had even painted the windowless bathroom adjacent to it a cheery red and yellow, and he had installed a portable shower. Every morning he would lock her in the bathroom, and while she was showering he would vacuum and scrub the secret place. He kept it immaculate. As he did everything in his life. He couldn't abide untidiness. He laid out clean clothes for her every day too. He also washed and ironed the clothes she came in, just as he had with the others. He had even had her jacket cleaned, that silly jacket with the names of cities all over the world. He didn't want to have it cleaned, but noticing that spot on the sleeve drove him crazy. He couldn't get it out of his head. Finally he gave in.

He spent a lot of money cleaning his own clothes as well. Sometimes when he woke up, he would find himself trying to brush away crumbs from the sheets. Was that because he remembered having to do that? There were a lot of questions from his childhood, things he couldn't fully remember. But maybe it was best that way.

He knew he was fortunate. He was able to spend all his time with the women he chose because he didn't have to work. He didn't need the money. His father had never spent a cent on anything besides bare essentials. After high school, when he began working for the builder, his father demanded he turn over his paycheck to him. "I'm saving for you, August," he had said. "It's wasteful to spend money on women. They're all like your mother. Taking everything you have and leaving with another man for California. Said she was too young when we got married, that nineteen was too young to have a baby. Not too young for *my* mother, I told her."

Ten years ago his father died suddenly, and he had been astonished to find that during all those years of penny-pinching, his father had invested in stocks. At thirty-four, he, August Mensch, was worth over a million dollars. Suddenly he could afford to travel and to live the way he wanted to, the way he had dreamed about during all those years of sitting at home at night, listening to his father tell him how his mother neglected him when he was a baby. "She left you in the playpen for hours. When you cried, she'd throw a bottle or some crackers to you. You were her prisoner, not her baby. I bought baby books, but she wouldn't even read to you. I'd come home from work and find you sitting in spilled milk and crumbs, cold and neglected."

August had moved to this place last year, rented this furnished and run-down town house cheaply, and made the necessary repairs himself. He had painted it and scrubbed the kitchen and bathrooms until they shone, and he cleaned the furniture and polished the floors daily. His lease ran out on May first, only twenty days from now. He had already told the owner he was planning to leave. By then he would have had Matthews and it would be time to move on. He would be leaving the place greatly improved. The only thing he would have to take care of was to whitewash all the improvements he had made to the secret place, so no one would ever guess what had happened there.

How many cities had he lived in during the last ten years? he wondered. He had lost track. Seven? Eight? More? Starting with finding his mother in San Diego. He liked Washington, would have stayed there longer. But he knew that after Bree Matthews it wouldn't be a good idea.

What kind of guest would she be? he wondered. Tiffany had been both frightened and angry. She ridiculed the books he bought for her, refusing to read to him. She told him her family had no money, as if that was what he wanted. She told him she wanted to paint. He even bought an easel and art supplies for her.

She actually started one painting while she was visiting, a painting of a man and woman kissing. It was going to be a copy of Klimt's *The Kiss*. He tore it off the easel and told her to copy one of the nice illustrations in the children's books he had given her. That was when she had picked up an open jar of paint and thrown it at him.

August Mensch didn't quite remember the next minutes, just that when he looked down at the sticky mess on his jacket and trousers, he had lunged at her.

When her body was pulled out of a Washington canal the next day, they questioned her ex-boyfriends. The papers were full of the case. He laughed at the speculation about where she had been the three weeks she was missing.

Mensch sighed. He didn't want to think of Tiffany now. He wanted to dust and polish the room again to make it ready for Matthews. Then he had to finish chiseling mortar from the cinder blocks in the wall that separated his basement from hers.

He would remove enough of those blocks to gain entry into Matthews' basement. He would bring her back the same way. He knew she had installed a security system, but this way it wouldn't do her any good. Then he would replace the cinder blocks and carefully re-cement.

It was Sunday night. He had watched her house all day. She hadn't gone out at all. Lately she had stayed in on Sundays, since Carter stopped coming around. He had seen him there last a couple of weeks ago.

He brushed away an invisible piece of dust. Tomorrow at this time she would be with him; she'd be his companion. He had bought a stack of Dr. Seuss books for her to read to him. He had thrown out all the other books. Some had been splattered with red paint. All of them reminded him how Tiffany had refused to read to him.

Over the years, he had always tried to make his guests comfortable. It wasn't his fault that they were always ungrateful. He remembered how the one in Kansas City told him she wanted a steak. He had bought a thick one, the thickest he could find. When he came back he could see that she had used the time he was out to try to escape. She hadn't wanted the steak at all. He'd lost his temper. He couldn't remember exactly what happened after that.

He hoped Bree would be nicer.

He'd soon know. Tomorrow morning he would make his move.

"What is *that?*" Bree muttered to herself as she stood at the head of the stairs leading to her basement. She could hear a faint scraping sound emanating from the basement of the adjacent town house.

She shook her head. What did it matter? She couldn't sleep anyway. It was irritating, though. Only six o'clock on a Monday morning, and Mensch was already on some do-it-yourself project. Some neat-as-a-pin improvement, no doubt, she said to herself, already in a bad temper.

She sighed. What a rotten day it was going to be. She had a lousy cold. There was no point getting up so early, but she wasn't sleepy. She had felt miserable yesterday and had stayed in bed all day, dozing. She hadn't even bothered to pick up the phone, just listened to messages. Her folks were away. Gran didn't call, and a certain Mr. Kevin Carter never put his finger on the touch tone.

Now cold or no cold, she was due in court at nine A.M. to try to make that first contractor pay for the repairs she had to do to the roof he was supposed to have fixed. To say nothing of getting him to pay for the damage inside caused by the leaks. She closed the basement door decisively and went into the kitchen, squeezed a grapefruit, made coffee, toasted an English muffin, settled at the breakfast bar.

She had begun to refer to this townhouse as the dwelling-from-hell, but once all the damage was repaired she had to admit it would be lovely.

She tried to eat her breakfast, but found she couldn't. I've never testified in court, she thought. That's why I'm nervous and down. But I'm sure the judge will side with me, she reassured herself. No judge would put up with having his or her house ruined.

Bree—short for Bridget—Matthews, thirty, single, blue-eyed and dark-haired, with porcelain skin that wouldn't tolerate the sun, was admittedly jumpy by nature. Buying this place last year had so far been an expensive mistake. For once I should *not* have listened to Granny, she thought, then smiled unconsciously thinking of how from her retirement community in Connecticut her grandmother still burned up the wires giving her good advice.

Eight years ago she was the one who told me I should take the job in Washington working for our congressman even though she thought he was a dope, Bree remembered as she forced herself to eat half of the English muffin. Then she advised me to grab the chance to join Douglas Public Relations when I got that offer. She's been right about everything except about buying this place and renovating it, Bree thought. "Real estate's a good way to make money, Bree," she had said, "especially in Georgetown."

Wrong! Bree frowned grimly as she sipped coffee. My Pierre Deux wall hangings are stained and peeling. And it's not wall*paper,* mind you, not when you spring for seventy dollars a yard. At that price the stuff becomes wall*hanging.* She frowned as she remembered explaining that to Kevin, who had said, "Now, that's what I call pretentious." Just what she needed to hear!

Mentally she reviewed everything she would tell the judge: "The Persian carpet that Granny proudly put on the floor of her first house is rolled and wrapped in plastic to be sure no new leaks can damage it further, and the polish on the parquet floors is dull and stained. I've got pictures to show just how bad my home looks. I wish you'd look at them, your honor. Now I'm waiting for the painter and floor guy to come back to charge a fortune to redo what they did perfectly well four months ago.

"I asked, pleaded, begged, even snarled at that contractor, trying to get him to take care of the leak. Then when he finally did show up, he told me that the water was coming from my neighbor's roof, and I believed him. I made a dope of myself ringing his bell, accusing poor Mr. Mensch of causing all the problems. You see, your honor, we share a common wall, and the contractor said the water was getting in that way. I, of course, believed him. He is supposed to be the expert."

Bree thought of her next-door neighbor, the balding guy with the graying ponytail who looked embarrassed just to say hello if they ran into each other on the street. The day that she had gone storming over, he had invited her in. At first he had listened to her rant with calm, unblinking eyes, his face thoughtful—as she imagined a priest would look during confession, if she could see through the screen, of course. Then he had suddenly started blushing and perspiring and almost whispered his protest that it couldn't be his roof, because surely he would have a leak too. She should call another contractor, he said.

"I scared the poor guy out of his wits," she had told Kevin that night. "I should have known the minute I saw the way he keeps his place that he'd never tolerate a leaking roof. The polish on the floor in his foyer almost blinded me. I bet when he was a kid he got a medal for being the neatest boy in camp."

Kevin. That was something else. Try as she might, she couldn't keep him from coming to mind. She would be seeing him this morning, the first time in a while. He had insisted on meeting her in court even though they were no longer dating.

I've never brought anyone to court, she thought, and going there is definitely not my idea of a good time, particularly since I absolutely do not want to see Kevin. Pouring herself a second cup of coffee, she settled back at the breakfast bar. Just because Kev helped me file the complaint, she thought, he's going to be Johnny-on-the-spot in court today, which thank you very much I don't need. I do not want to see him. At all. And it's such a gloomy day all around. Bree looked out the window at the thick fog. She shook her head, her mouth set in a hard line. In fact, her irritation with Kevin had become so pronounced she practically blamed him for the leaking roof. He no longer called every morning, or sent flowers on the seventeenth of every month, the seventeenth being the day on which they had their first date. That was ten months ago, just after Bree had moved in to the town house. Bree felt the hard line of her mouth turning down at the corners, and she shook her head again. I love being independent, she thought ruefully, but sometimes I hate being alone.

Bree knew she had to get over all this. She realized that she was getting in the habit of regularly rearguing her quarrel with Kevin Carter. She also realized that when she missed him most—like this past Saturday, when she had moped around, going to a movie and having dinner alone, or yesterday when she stayed in bed feeling lonely and lousy—she needed to reinforce her sense of being in the right.

Bree remembered their fight, which like most had started out small and soon took on epic, life-changing proportions. Kev said I was foolish not to accept the settlement the contractor offered me, she recalled, that I probably won't get much more by going to court, but I wouldn't think of it. I'm pigheaded and love a fight and always shoot from the hip. Telling me that I was becoming irrational about this, he said that, for example, I had no business storming next door after that shy little guy. I reminded him that I apologized profusely, and Mr. Mensch was so sweet about it that he even offered to fix that broken blind in the living room window.

Somewhat uncomfortably, Bree remembered that there had been a pause in their exchange, but instead of letting it go, she had then told Kevin that he seemed to be the one who loved a fight, and why did he have to always take everybody else's side? That was when he said maybe we should step back and examine our relationship. And I said that if it has to be examined, then it didn't exist, so good-bye.

She sighed. It had been a very long two weeks.

I really wish Mensch would stop that damn tinkering or whatever he's doing in his basement, she thought, hearing the noise again. Lately he had been

50

giving her the creeps. She had seen him watching her when she got out of the car, and she had felt his eyes following her whenever she moved about her yard. Maybe he did take offense that day and is brooding about it, she reasoned. She had been thinking about telling Kevin that Mensch was making her nervous—but then they had the quarrel, and she never got the chance. Anyway, Mensch seemed harmless enough.

Bree shrugged, then got up, still holding her coffee cup. I'm just all around jumpy, she thought, but in a couple of hours this will be behind me, one way or the other. Tonight I'll come home early, go to bed and sleep off this damn cold, and tomorrow I'll start to get the house in shipshape again.

Again the scraping sound came from the basement. Knock it off, she almost said aloud. Briefly debating going down to see what was causing the noise, she decided against it. So Mensch has a do-it-yourself project going, she thought. It's none of my business.

Then the scraping noise stopped, followed by hollow silence. Was that a footstep on the basement stairs? Impossible. The basement door that led outside was bolted and armed. Then what was causing it? . . .

She whirled around to see her next-door neighbor standing behind her, a hypodermic needle in his hand.

As she dropped the coffee cup, he plunged the needle deep into her arm.

Kevin Carter, *J.D.*, felt the level of his irritability hit the danger zone. This was just another example of Bree's total inability to listen to reason, he thought. She's pigheaded. Strong-willed. Impulsive. So where in hell was she?

The contractor, Richie Omberg, had shown up on time. A surly-looking guy, he kept looking at his watch and mumbling about being due on a job. He raised his voice as he reiterated his position to his lawyer: "I offered to fix the leak, but by then she'd had it done at six times what I coulda done it for. Twice I'd sent someone to look at it and she wasn't home. Once the guy who inspected it said he thought it was coming from the next roof, said there hasta be a leak there. Guess that little squirt who rented next door fixed it. Anyhow, I offered to pay what it woulda cost me."

Bree had been due in court at nine o'clock. When she hadn't shown up by ten, the judge dismissed the complaint.

A furious Kevin Carter went to his job at the State Department. He did not call Bridget Matthews at Douglas Public Relations where she worked, nor did he attempt to call her at home. The next call between them was going to come from her. She owed him an apology. He tried not to remember that after she had gotten her day in court, he had planned to tell her that he missed her like hell and please, let's make up.

Mensch dragged Bree's limp body through the kitchen to the hallway that led to the basement stairs. He slid her down, step by step, until he reached the bottom; then he bent down and picked her up. Clearly she hadn't bothered to do anything with her basement. The cinder-block walls were gray and dreary, the floor tiles were clean but shabby. He had made the opening in the wall in the boiler room where it would be least noticed. He had pulled the cinder blocks into his basement, so now all he had to do was to secure her in the secret place, come back to get her clothing, then replace and re-mortar the blocks.

The opening he had made was just large enough to slide her body through and then crawl in after her. In his basement he picked her up again and carried her to the secret place. She was still knocked out, so there was no resistance as he attached the restraints to her wrists and ankles, and, as a precaution, tied the scarf loosely around her mouth. He could tell from her breathing that she had a cold. He certainly didn't want her to suffocate.

For a moment he reveled in the sight of her, limp and lovely, her hair tumbling onto the mattress, her body relaxed and peaceful. He straightened her terry-cloth robe and tucked it around her.

Now that she was here, he felt so strong, so calm. He had been shocked to find her in the kitchen so early in the morning. Now he had to move quickly: to get her clothes and her purse, to wipe up that spilled coffee. It had to look as if she disappeared after she left the house.

He looked at the answering machine in her kitchen, the blinking light indicating there had been seven calls. That was odd, he thought. He knew she hadn't gone out at all yesterday. Was it possible she didn't bother to answer the phone all day?

He played the messages back. All calls from friends. "How are you?" "Let's get together." "Good luck in court." "Hope you make that contractor pay." The last message was from the same person as the first: "Guess you're still out. I'll try you tomorrow."

Mensch took a moment to sit down at the breakfast bar. It was very important that he think all this through. Matthews had not gone out at all yesterday.

It seemed as though she also hadn't answered her phone all day. Suppose instead of just taking her clothes to make it look as though she'd left for work, I tidied up the house so that people would think she hadn't reached home at all on Saturday night. After all, he had seen her come up the block alone at around eleven, the newspaper under her arm. Who was there to say she had arrived safely?

Mensch got up. He already had his Latex gloves on. He started looking about. The garbage container under the kitchen sink was empty. He took a fresh disposable bag from the drawer and put in it the squeezed grapefruit, coffee grinds, and pieces of the cup Bree had dropped.

Working methodically, he cleaned the kitchen, even taking time to scour the pot she had left on the stove. How careless of her to let it get burned, he thought.

Upstairs in her bedroom, he made the bed and picked up the Sunday edition of the *Washington Post* that was on the floor next to it. He put the paper in the garbage bag. She had left a suit on the bed. He hung it up in the closet where she kept that kind of clothing.

Next he cleaned the bathroom. Her washer and dryer were in the bathroom, concealed by louvered doors. On top of the washer he found the jeans and sweater he had seen her wearing on Saturday. It hadn't started raining at the time, but she had also had on her yellow raincoat. He collected the sweater and jeans and her undergarments and sneakers and socks. Then from her dresser he selected more undergarments. From her closets he took a few pairs of slacks and sweaters. They were basically nondescript, and he knew they would never be missed.

He found her raincoat and shoulder bag in the foyer by the front door. Mensch looked at his watch. It was seven thirty, time to go. He had to replace and re-mortar the cinder blocks.

He looked around to be sure he had missed nothing. His eye fell on the lopsided venetian blind in the front window. A knifelike pain went through his skull; his gorge rose. He felt almost physically ill. He couldn't stand to look at it.

Mensch put the clothing and purse and garbage bag on the floor. In quick, determined steps he reached the window and put his gloved hand on the blind.

The cord was broken, but there was enough slack to tie it and still level the blind.

He breathed a long sigh of relief when he finished the task. It now stopped at exactly the same level as the other two and as his, just grazing the sill.

He felt much better now. With neat, compact movements he gathered up Bree's coat, shoulder bag, clothing, and the garbage bag.

Two minutes later he was in his own basement, replacing the cinder blocks.

At first Bree thought she was having a nightmare— a Disney World nightmare. When she woke up she opened her eyes to see cinder-block walls painted with evenly spaced brown slats. The space was small, not much more than six by nine feet, and she was lying on a bright yellow plastic mattress of some sort. It was soft, as though it had quilts inside it. About three feet from the ceiling a band of yellow paint connected the slats at the top to resemble a railing. Above the band, decals lined the walls: Mickey Mouse. Cinderella. Kermit the Frog. Miss Piggy. Sleeping Beauty. Poca-hontas.

She suddenly realized that there was a gag over her face, and she tried to push it away, but could only move her arm a few inches. Her arms and legs were held in some kind of restraints.

The grogginess was lifting now. Where was she? What had happened? Panic overwhelmed her as she remembered turning to see Mensch, her neighbor, standing behind her in the kitchen. Where had he taken her? Where was he now?

She looked around slowly, then her eyes widened. This room, wherever it was, resembled an oversized playpen. Stacked nearby were a series of children's books, all with thin spines except for the thick volume at the bottom. She could read the lettering: *Grimm's Fairy Tales.*

How had she gotten here? She remembered she had been about to get dressed to go to court. She had tossed the suit she had planned to wear across the bed. It was new. She wanted to look good, and in truth, more for Kevin than for the judge. Now she admitted that much to herself.

Kevin. Of course he would come looking for her when she didn't show up in court. He'd know something had happened to her.

Ica, her housekeeper, would look for her too. She came in on Mondays. She'd know something was wrong. Bree remembered dropping the coffee cup she was holding. It shattered on the kitchen floor as Mensch grabbed her and stuck the needle in her arm. Ica would know that she wouldn't leave spilled coffee and a broken cup for her to clean up.

As her head cleared, Bree remembered that just before she had turned and seen Mensch, she had heard a footstep on the basement stairs. Her mouth went dry at the thought that somehow he had come in through the basement. But how? Her basement door was bolted and armed, the window barred.

Then sheer panic swept through her. Clearly this hadn't just "happened"; this had been carefully planned. She tried to scream, but could only make a muffled gasping cry. She tried to pray, a single sentence that in her soul she repeated over and over: *"Please, God, let Kevin find me."*

Late Tuesday afternoon Kevin received a worried phone call from the agency where Bree worked. Had he heard from her? She never showed up for work on Monday, and she hadn't phoned. They thought she might have been stuck in court all day yesterday, but now they were concerned.

Fifteen minutes later, August Mensch watched through a slit in his front window drapery as Kevin Carter held his finger on the doorbell to Bree Matthews' town house.

He watched as Carter stood on the front lawn and looked in the living room window. He half expected that Carter would ring his doorbell, but that didn't happen. Instead he stood for a few minutes looking irresolute, then looked in the window of the garage. Mensch knew her car was there. In a way he wished he could have gotten rid of it, but that had been impossible.

He watched until Carter, his shoulders slumped, walked slowly back to his car and drove away.

With a satisfied smile, Mensch walked down the foyer to the basement steps. Savoring the sight that would greet him, he descended slowly, then walked across the basement, as always admiring his tools and paints and polishes, all placed in perfect order on shelves, or hanging in precise rows from neatly squared pegboard.

Snow shovels hung over the cinder blocks that he

had removed to gain entry into Matthews' basement. Beneath them the mortar had dried, and he had carefully smeared it with the dry flakes he had kept when he separated the blocks. Now nothing showed, either here on or Bridget Matthews' side. He was sure of that.

Then he crossed through the boiler room, and beyond it, to the secret place.

Matthews was lying on the mat, the restraints still on her arms and legs. She looked up at him and he could see that underneath the anger, fear was beginning to take hold. That was smart of her.

She was wearing a sweater and slacks, things he had taken from her closet.

He knelt before her and removed the gag from her mouth. It was a silk scarf, tied so that it was neither too tight nor caused a mark. "Your boyfriend was just looking for you," he told her. "He's gone now."

He loosened the restraints on her left arm and leg. "What book would you like to read to me today, Mommy?" he asked, his voice suddenly childlike and begging.

On Thursday morning Kevin sat in the office of FBI agent Lou Ferroni. The nation's capital was awash with cherry blossoms, but as he stared out the window he was unaware of them. Everything seemed a blur, especially the last two days: his frantic call to the police, the questions, the calls to Bree's family, the calls to friends, the sudden involvement of the FBI. What was Ferroni saying? Kevin forced himself to listen.

"She's been gone long enough for us to consider her a missing person," the agent said. Fifty-three years old and nearing retirement, Ferroni realized that he'd seen the look on Carter's face far too often in the past twenty-eight years, always on the faces of those left behind. Shock. Fear. Heartsick that the person they love may not be alive.

Carter was the boyfriend, or ex-boyfriend. He'd freely admitted that he and Matthews had quarreled. Ferroni wasn't eliminating him as a suspect, but he seemed unlikely and his alibi checked out. Bridget, or Bree, as her friends called her, had been in her house on Saturday, that much they knew. They had not been able to locate anyone who saw or spoke to her on Sunday, though, and she hadn't shown up for her court appointment on Monday.

"Let's go over it again," Ferroni suggested. "You say that Miss Matthews' housekeeper was surprised to find the bed made and dishes done when she came in Monday morning?" He had already spoken with the housekeeper, but wanted to see if there were any discrepancies in Carter's story.

Kevin nodded. "I called Ica as soon as I realized Bree was missing. She has a key to Bree's place. I picked her up and she let me in. Of course Bree wasn't there. Ica told me that when she went in on Monday morning she couldn't understand why the bed was made and the dishes run through in the dishwasher. It just wasn't normal. Bree never made the bed on Monday because that was when Ica changed it. So that meant the bed had not been slept in Sunday night, and that Bree could have vanished any time between Saturday and Sunday night."

Ferroni's gut instinct told him that the misery he was seeing in Kevin Carter's face was genuine. So if he didn't do it, who did that leave? Richie Ombert, the contractor Matthews was suing, had had several complaints filed against him for using abusive language and threatening gestures toward disgruntled customers.

Certainly the renovation business caused tempers to flare. Ferroni knew that firsthand. His wife had been ready to practically murder the guy who built the addition on their house. Ombert, though, seemed worse than most. He had a nasty edge, and for the moment he was a prime suspect in Bridget Matthews' disappearance.

There was one aspect of this case Ferroni was not prepared to share with Carter. The computer of VICAP, the FBI's violent criminal apprehension program, had been tracking a particular pattern of disappearing young women. The trail started some ten years ago in California, when a young art student disappeared. Her body showed up three weeks later; she had been strangled. The weird part was that when she was found she was dressed in the same clothes as when she had disappeared, and they were freshly washed and pressed. There was no sign of molestation, no hint of violence beyond the obvious cause of death. But where had she been those three weeks?

Shortly afterwards the VICAP computer spat out a case in Arizona with striking similarities. One followed in New Mexico, then Colorado . . . North Dakota . . . Wisconsin . . . Kansas . . . Missouri . . . Indiana . . . Ohio . . . Pennsylvania. . . . Finally, six months ago, there in D.C., an art student, Tiffany Wright, had disappeared. Her body was fished out of a Washington canal three weeks later, but it had been there only a short time. Except for the effect the water had had on her clothes, they were neat. The only odd note were some faint spots of red paint, the kind artists use, still visible on her blouse.

That little clue had started them working on the art

student angle, looking among her classmates. It was the first time there had been any kind of stain or mark or rip or tear on any of the women's clothes. So far, however, it had led nowhere. Odds were that the disappearance of Bridget Matthews was not tied to the death of Tiffany Wright. It would be a marked departure in the serial killer's method of operation for him to strike twice in one city, but then maybe he was changing his habits.

"By any chance is Miss Matthews interested in art?" Ferroni asked Carter. "Does she take art lessons as a hobby?"

Kevin kneaded his forehead, trying to relieve the ache that reminded him of the one time in his life he had had too much to drink.

Bree, where are you?

"She never took art lessons that I know of. Bree was more into music and the theater," he said. "We went to Kennedy Center pretty frequently. She particularly liked concerts."

Liked? he thought. Why am I using the past tense? No, God, no!

Ferroni consulted the notes in his hand. "Kevin, I want to go over this again. It's important. You were familiar with the house. There may be something you noticed when you went in with the housekeeper."

Kevin hesitated.

"What is it?" Ferroni asked quickly.

Through haggard eyes, Kevin stared at him. Then he glumly shook his head. "There *was* something different; I sensed it at the time. But I don't know what it was."

How many days have I been here? Bree asked herself. She had lost count. Three? Five? They were all blending together. Mensch had just gone upstairs with her breakfast tray. She knew he'd be back within the hour for her to begin reading to him again.

He had a routine he followed rigidly. In the morning, he came down carrying fresh clothing for her, a blouse or sweater, jeans or slacks. Obviously he had taken the time to go through her closet and dresser after he had knocked her out. It appeared that he had only brought casual clothes that were washable.

Next he would unshackle her hands, connect the leg restraints to each other at the ankles, then lead her to the bathroom, drop the clean clothes on a chair, and lock her in. A minute later she'd hear the whir of the vacuum.

She had studied him closely. He was thin but strong. No matter how she tried to think of a way to escape, she was sure she couldn't manage it. The ankle restraints forced her to shuffle a few feet at a time, so she clearly couldn't outrun him. There was nothing that she could use to stun him long enough for her to get up the stairs and out the door.

She knew where she was—the basement of his town house. The wall on the right was the one that they shared. She thought of how upset she had been about the stained wallpaper on that wall. No, not wall*paper*—wall*hanging,* Bree reminded herself, fighting back an hysterical wave of laughter.

By now the police are looking for me, she thought. Kevin will tell them how I accused Mensch of causing the leak in the roof. They'll investigate him, then they'll realize there's something weird about him. Surely they can't miss that?

Will Mom and Dad tell Gran that I'm missing? Please God, don't let them tell her. It would be too much of a shock for her.

She had to believe that somehow the police would start to investigate Mensch. It seemed so obvious that he must have kidnapped her. Surely they would figure it out? But, of course, trapped here in this cell she had no idea what anyone outside might be thinking. Someone would have missed her by now—she was certain of that—but where were they looking? She had absolutely no idea, and unless Mensch radically altered his routine, there would be no opportunity to let them know she was here. No, she would just have to wait and hope. And stay alive. To stay alive she had to keep him appeased until help came. As long as she read the children's books to him, he seemed to be satisfied.

Last night she had given him a list of books by Roald Dahl that he should get. He had been pleased. "None of my guests were as nice as you," he told her.

What had he *done* to those women? Don't think about that, Bree warned herself fiercely—it worries him when you show that you're afraid. She had realized that the one time she broke down sobbing and begged him to release her. That was when he told her that the police had rung his bell and asked when the last time was that he had seen Miss Matthews.

"I told them I was on my way back from the supermarket Saturday, around two o'clock, and I saw you go out. They asked what you were wearing. I said it was overcast and you had on a bright yellow raincoat and slacks. They thanked me and said I was very helpful," he said calmly, in his sing-song voice.

That was when she became almost hysterical.

"You're making too much noise," he told her. He put one hand on her mouth, while the other encircled her throat. For a moment she thought he was going to strangle her. But then he hesitated and said, "Promise to be quiet, and I'll let you read to me. Please, Mommy, don't cry."

Since then she had managed to hold her emotion in check.

Bree steeled herself. She could sense that he'd be back any moment. Then she heard it, the turning of the handle. Oh, God, please, she prayed, let them find me.

Mensch came in. She could see that he looked troubled. "My landlord phoned," he told her. "He said that according to the contract he has the right to show this place two weeks before the lease is up. That's Monday, and it's Friday already. And I have to take all the decorations down from here and white-wash the walls and also the walls of the bathroom and give them time to dry. That will take the whole weekend. So this has to be our last day together, Bridget. I'm sorry. I'll go out and buy some more books, but I guess you should try to read to me a little faster . . ."

At ten o'clock on Friday morning, Kevin was once again in Lou Ferroni's office in the FBI building.

"Thanks to the publicity, we've been able to pretty much cover Miss Matthews' activities on Saturday," Agent Ferroni told him. "Several neighbors reported they saw her walking down the street at about two o'clock on Saturday. They agree that she was wearing a bright yellow raincoat and jeans and carrying a shoulder bag. We know the raincoat and bag are missing from her home. We don't know what she did on Saturday afternoon, but we do know she had dinner alone at Antonio's in Georgetown and went to the nine o'clock showing of the new Batman film at the Beacon Theater."

Bree had dinner alone on Saturday night, Kevin thought. So did I. And she genuinely likes those crazy Batman films. We've laughed about that. I can't stand them, but I had promised to see that one with her.

"No one seems to have seen Miss Matthews after that," Ferroni continued. "But we do have one piece of information that we find significant. We've learned that the contractor she was suing was in the same movie theater that night at the same showing. He claims he drove directly home, but there's no one to back up his story. He apparently separated from his wife recently."

Ferroni did not add that the contractor had mouthed off to a number of people about what he'd like to do to the dame who was hauling him into court over what he termed "some silly leak."

"We're working on the theory that Miss Matthews did not get home that night. Was she in the habit of using the Metro instead of her car?"

"The Metro or a cab if she was going directly from place to place. She said trying to park was too much of a nuisance." Kevin could see that Ferroni was starting to believe that Richie Ombert, the contractor, was responsible for Bree's disappearance. He thought of Ombert in court this past Monday. Surly. Aggravated. Noisily elated when the judge dismissed the complaint.

He wasn't acting, Kevin thought. He seemed genuinely surprised and relieved when Bree didn't show up. No, Ombert is not the answer. He shook his head, trying to clear it. He suddenly felt as though he were being smothered. He had to get out of here. "There are no other leads?" he asked Ferroni.

The FBI agent thought of the briefly considered theory that Bree Matthews had been abducted by a serial killer. "No," he said firmly, then added, "How is Miss Matthews' family? Has her father gone back to Connecticut?"

"He had to. We're in constant touch, but Bree's grandmother had a mild heart attack Tuesday evening. One of those horrible coincidences. Bree's mother is with her. You can imagine the state she's in. That's why Bree's father went back."

Ferroni shook his head. "I'm sorry. I wish I thought we'd get good news." He realized that in a way it would have been better if they thought the serial killer had Matthews. All the women he had abducted had lived for several weeks after disappearing. That would at least give them more time.

Kevin got up. "I'm going to Bree's house," he said. "I'm going to call every one of the people in her phone book."

Ferroni raised his eyebrows.

"I want to see if anyone spoke to her on Sunday," Kevin said simply.

"With all the publicity these last few days about her disappearance, any friend who spoke to her would have come forward, I'm sure of that," Ferroni told him. "How do you think we traced her movements on Saturday?"

Kevin did not answer.

"What about her answering machine? Were there any messages on it?" Kevin asked.

"Not from Sunday, or if there had been, they were erased," Ferroni replied. "At first we thought it might be significant, but then we realized that she could have called in and gotten them just by using the machine's code."

Kevin shook his head dejectedly. He had to get out

of there. He had promised to phone Ica after his meeting with Ferroni but decided to wait and call her from Bree's house instead. He realized he was frantic to be there, that somehow being around her things made him feel nearer to Bree.

Her neighbor, the guy with the ponytail, was coming down the block when Kevin parked in front of the house. He was carrying a shopping bag from the bookstore. Their eyes met, but neither man spoke. Instead the neighbor nodded, then turned to go up his walk.

Wouldn't you think he'd have the decency to at least *ask* about Bree? Kevin thought bitterly. Too damn busy washing his windows or tending his lawn to give a damn about anyone else.

Or maybe he's embarrassed to ask. Afraid of what he'll hear. Kevin took out the key Ica had given him, let himself in to the house, and phoned her.

"Can you come over and help me?" he asked. "There's something about this place that's bugging me. Something's just not quite right, and I can't figure out what it is. Maybe you can help."

While he waited, he stared at the phone. Bree was one of the few women he had ever known who considered the phone an intrusion. "At home we always turned off the ringer at mealtime," she had told him. "It's so much more civilized."

So civilized that now we don't know if anyone spoke to you on Sunday, Kevin thought. He looked around; there's got to be a clue here somewhere, he told himself. Why was he so sure that the contractor wasn't the answer to Bree's disappearance?

Restlessly he began to walk around the downstairs floor. He stopped at the door of the front room. The contrast to the cheery kitchen and den was striking. Here as in the dining room, because of the water damage, the furniture and carpet were covered with plastic and pushed to the center of the room.

The wallpaper—or wall*hanging* (as Bree had insisted it be called)—a soft ivory with a faint stripe, was stained and bubbled.

Kevin remembered how happy Bree had been when all the decorating was supposedly finished three months ago. They'd even talked around the subject of marriage, in the same sentence mentioning her town house and the marvelous old farmhouse he had bought for Virginia weekends.

Too damn cautious to commit ourselves, Kevin thought bitterly. But not too cautious to have a fight over nothing. It had all been so silly.

He thought about sitting with her in that same room, the warm ivories and reds and blues of the Persian carpet repeated up in the newly reupholstered couch and chairs. Bree had pointed to the vertical metal blinds.

"I hate those damn things," she had said. "The last one doesn't even close properly, but I wanted to get everything else in before I choose draperies."

The blinds. He looked up.

The doorbell rang, interrupting his train of thought. It was Ica. The handsome Jamaican woman's face mirrored the misery he felt. "I haven't slept two hours straight this week," she said. "Looks to me as though you haven't either."

Kevin nodded. "Ica, there's something about this house that's bothering me, something I ought to be noticing. Help me."

She nodded. "It's funny you should say that, 'cause

I felt that way too, but blamed it on finding the bed being made and the dishes done. But if Bree didn't get home Saturday night, then that would explain those things. She never left the place untidy."

Together they walked up the stairs to the bedroom. Ica looked around uncertainly. "The room felt different when I got here Monday, different from the way it usually feels," she said hesitantly.

"In what way?" Kevin asked quickly.

"It was . . . well, it was way too neat." Ica walked over to the bed. "Those throw pillows, Bree just tossed them around, like the way they are now."

"What are you telling me?" Kevin asked. He grabbed her arm, aware that Ica was about to tell him what he needed to know.

"This whole place felt just—too neat. I stripped the bed even though it was made because I wanted to change the sheets. I had to dig and pull the sheets and blanket loose, they were tucked in so tight. And the throw pillows on top of the quilt were all lined up against the headboard like little soldiers."

"Anything else? Please just keep talking, Ica. We may be getting somewhere," Kevin begged.

"Yes," Ica said excitedly. "Last week Bree had let a pot boil over. I scoured it as best I could and left a note for her to pick up some steel wool and scouring powder; I said I'd finish it when I came back. Monday morning that pot was sitting out on the stove, scrubbed clean as could be. I know my Bree. She never would have touched it. She told me those strong soaps made her hands break out. Come on, I'll show it to you."

Together they ran down the stairs into the kitchen. From the cupboard she pulled out a gleaming pot.

"There isn't even a mark on the bottom," she said. "You'd think it was practically brand new." She looked excitedly at Kevin. "Things just weren't right here. The bed was made too neatly. This pot is too clean."

"And . . . and the blind in the front window has been fixed," Kevin shouted. "It's lined up like the ones next door."

He didn't know he had been about to say that, but suddenly he realized that was what had been bothering him all along. He had sensed the difference right away, but the effect had been so subtle, it had registered only in his subconscious. But now that he had brought it into focus, he thought of the neighbor, the quiet guy with the ponytail, the one who was always washing his windows or trimming his lawn or sweeping his walk.

What did anyone know about him? If he rang the bell, Bree might have let him in. And he had offered to fix the blind—Bree had mentioned that. Kevin pulled Ferroni's card from his pocket and handed it to Ica. "I'm going next door. Tell Ferroni to get over here fast."

"Just one more book. That's all we'll have time for. Then you'll leave me again, Mommy. Just like she did. Just like all of them did."

In the two hours she had been reading to him, Bree had watched Mensch regress from adoring to angry child. He's working up the courage to kill me, she thought.

He was sitting cross-legged beside her on the mat.

"But I want to read *all* of them to you," she said, her voice soothing, coaxing. "I know you'll love them.

70

Then tomorrow I could help you to paint the walls. We could get it done so much faster if we work together. Then we could go away somewhere together, so I can keep reading to you."

He stood up abruptly. "You're trying to trick me. You don't want to go with me. You're just like all the others." He stared at her, his eyes shuttered and small with anger. "I saw your boyfriend go into your house a little while ago. He's too nosy. It's good that you're wearing the jeans. I have to get your raincoat and shoulder bag." He looked as if he was about to cry. "There's no time for any more books," he said sadly.

He rushed out. I'm going to die, Bree thought. Frantically she tried to pull her arms and legs free of the restraints. Her right arm swung up and she realized that he'd forgotten to refasten the shackle to the wall. He had said Kevin was next door. She had heard that you can transfer thoughts. She closed her eyes and concentrated: *Kevin, help me. Kevin, I need you.*

She had to play for time. She would have only one chance at him, one moment of surprise. She would swing at his head with the dangling shackle, try to stun him. But what good would that do? Save her for a few seconds? *Then* what? she thought despondently. How could she stop him?

Her eyes fell on the stack of books. Maybe there was a way. She grabbed the first one and began tearing the pages, scattering the pieces, forcing them to flutter hither and yon across the bright yellow mattress.

I must have known that today was the day, Mensch thought as he retrieved Bree's raincoat and shoulder bag from the bedroom closet. I laid out jeans and the red sweater she was wearing that Saturday. When they find her it will be like all the others. And again they will ask that same question: Where was she for the days she had been missing? It would be fun to read about it. Everyone wanting to know, and only he would have the answer.

As he came down the stairs, he stopped suddenly. The doorbell was ringing. The button was being held down. He laid down the pocketbook and the coat and stood frozen momentarily with uncertainty. Should he answer? Would it seem suspicious if he didn't? No. Better to get rid of her, get her out of here fast, he decided.

Mensch picked up the raincoat and rushed down the basement stairs.

I know he's in there, Kevin thought, but he's not answering. I've got to get inside.

Ica was running across the lawn. "Mr. Ferroni is on his way. He said to absolutely wait for him. Not to ring the bell anymore. He got all excited when I talked about everything being so neat. He said if it's what he thinks it is, Bree will still be alive."

It seemed to Kevin that he could hear Bree crying out to him. He was overwhelmed by a sense of running out of time, by an awareness that he had to get into Mensch's house immediately. He ran to the front window and strained to look in. Through the slats he could see the rigidly neat living room. Craning his head, he could see the stairway in the foyer. Then his blood froze. A woman's leather shoulder bag was on the last step. Bree's shoulder bag! He recognized it; he had given it to her for her birthday.

Frantically he ran to the sidewalk where a refuse

can stood waiting to be emptied. He dumped the contents onto the street, ran back with the can, and overturned it under the window. As Ica steadied it for him, he climbed up, then kicked in the window. As the glass shattered, he kicked away the knifelike edges and jumped into the room. He raced up the stairs, shouting Bree's name.

Finding no one there, he clattered down the stairs again, pausing only long enough to open the front door. "Tell the FBI I'm inside, Ica."

He raced through the rooms on the ground floor and still found no one.

There was only one place left to search: the basement.

Finally the ringing stopped. Whoever had been at the door had gone away. Mensch knew he had to hurry. The raincoat and a plastic bag over his arm, he strode across the basement, through the boiler room, and opened the door to the secret room.

Then he froze. Bits of paper littered the yellow plastic. Matthews was tearing up the books, his baby books. "Stop it!" he shrieked.

His head hurt, his throat was closing. He had a pain in his chest. The room was a mess; he had to clean it up.

He felt dizzy, almost as if he couldn't breathe. It was as if the mess of papers was smothering him! He had to clean it up so he could breathe!

Then he would kill her. Kill her slowly. He ran into the bathroom, grabbed the wastebasket, ran back and began scooping up the shredded paper and mangled books. His frenzied hands worked quickly, efficiently. In only minutes there wasn't a single scrap left.

He looked about him. Matthews was cowering against the mattress. He stood over her. "You're a pig, just like my mommy. This is what I did to her." He knelt beside her, the plastic bag in his hands. Then her hand swung up. The shackle on her wrist slammed into his face.

He screamed, and for an instant he was stunned, then with a snarl he snapped his fingers around her throat.

The basement was empty too. Where was she? Kevin thought desperately. He was about to run into the garage, when from somewhere behind the boiler room he heard Mensch howl in pain. And then there came a scream. A woman's scream. Bree was screaming!

An instant later, as August Mensch tightened his hands on Bree Matthew's neck, he felt his head yanked back and then there was a violent punch that caused his knees to buckle. Dazed, he shook his head and then with a guttural cry sprang to his feet.

Bree reached out and grabbed his ankle, pulling him off balance as Kevin caught him in a hammer grip around the throat.

Moments later, pounding feet on the basement stairs announced the arrival of the FBI. One minute later Bree, now in the shelter of Kevin's arms, watched as Mensch was manacled with chains at his waist and hands and legs, looking dazed.

"Let's see how *you* like being tied up," she screamed at him.

Two days later, Bree and Kevin stood together at her grandmother's bedside in Connecticut. "The doctor said you'll be fine, Gran," Bree told her.

"Of course I'm fine. Forget the health talk. Let's hear about your place. I bet you made that contractor squirm in court, didn't you?"

Bree grinned at Kevin's raised eyebrows. "Oh, Gran, I decided to accept his settlement offer after all. I've finally realized that I really hate getting into fights."

Too Many Cooks

Carol Higgins Clark

Ellie Butternut had had quite the day, and it was only 2:05 in the afternoon. Three auditions for acting jobs, none of which she felt she was remotely right for, had eaten up the last five hours of her life. And she needed to land something before the end of the month. Something that would fall under the jurisdiction of the Screen Actors Guild so she would make the minimum amount required to keep herself hooked up to their health insurance plan.

She pulled her beat-up Honda in front of her not quite decaying apartment building in West Hollywood and stopped. It was street-cleaning day, and the parking regulations had been lifted five minutes before, which meant she wouldn't have to go through the shenanigans of parallel parking and squeezing in between two other clunkers. The street was free and clear, the Hollywood Hills visible in the distance beyond Sunset Boulevard and the local 7-Eleven.

She opened the car door, and the hot Los Angeles air blasted her in the face. Her car might not have looked the greatest, but thank God the air-conditioning worked. The midafternoon sun was doing a good job of beating its way down through the smog. Driplets of perspiration popped from her fore-head as Ellie hoisted her tote bag, loaded up with a lot of "just in case" items, over her shoulder. She often thought she would have made a good contestant on *Let's Make a Deal.* When Monty Hall came walking down the aisle asking if anyone had items such as a tape measure or a staple gun, Ellie could have pro-duced them and been rewarded with cash.

Ellie had actually been on a couple of game shows since she'd moved to Los Angeles after college twelve years before, in pursuit of her dream to become a successful comedic character actress. On one she'd scored big, winning over six thousand dollars. On the other she'd walked away with Lee Press-On Nails, a dozen cartons of macaroni noodles, and a lot of frustration for not guessing the word "anchor" when her celebrity contestant's clue was "ship."

I'm still waiting for my *ship to come in,* Ellie thought. Most of the last twelve years, besides her stints on game shows, had been spent working at odd jobs, with some acting work in industrials, commer-cials, and offbeat plays. There was also her acting class two nights a week, which she loved. But she was still searching for that one great part that would give her career a much-needed jolt. She also wouldn't mind if Mr. Right somehow showed up.

The walkway to her building was really a big piece of cracked cement, its crevices squiggling out in several different directions. Ellie often thought that if you plopped it in front of a luxury high rise, they'd call it modern art. Here it should be roped off with signs surrounding it: "Danger, you might trip."

At the locked and barred gate in front of her ground-floor apartment—the security devices had been installed after the neighbor upstairs was burglarized—Ellie grabbed the advertising circulars and menus that had been wrapped around the bars since morning and seemed to multiply faster than ants at a picnic. She stuffed them in her black bag.

Ellie unlocked the gate, pulled open her screen door, unlocked her front door, and gave it a shove. As usual, the sight of her cool shaded apartment with its white stucco walls and muted mauve furniture soothed her. She picked up the mail from the floor, straightened up her slightly overweight body, and pushed back the red curls from her forehead.

The next welcome sight was the red blinking light on her answering machine, which meant that some-body had cared enough to dial her number. The tiny screen indicated that there was one message.

"It only takes one," Ellie said as she pushed the playback button.

She was rewarded with a call from her agent.

"Ellie, this is Artie. You might find this remarkable, but I got you a job. And you don't even have to audition. It's playing a chef in a commercial for some new kind of steak sauce. They're filming up the coast in a big old restaurant on the water near San Luis Obispo. You've got to get up there tonight. The whole project has been plagued with problems. The actress they hired backed out because she's a vegetarian and decided at the last minute it was bad karma to hawk steak sauce. I'm glad I'm not her agent. Anyway, the director remembers you from the commercial you did for the cockroach spray. I know that whole thing didn't work out the greatest, with the bug spray making you break out in hives and the commercial never making it to the air, but he thought you were very effective and believable fighting those bugs. Give me a call as soon as you get this."

Ellie clapped her hands with delight and picked up the phone. "Me play a chef?" she said to herself as she pressed the automatic dial for Artie's office. "I can barely boil water."

Two hours later Ellie's Honda was chugging up the sometimes hilly coastal highway of California, heading north. The production company would have flown her up, but the flights weren't convenient and she preferred taking her own car. After the shoot, she'd drive over to her cousin Peter's house for dinner and spend the night. He was married with two kids and lived a normal, secure life in San Luis Obispo. Whenever Ellie visited, he and his wife enjoyed listening to her horror stories of both her personal and professional life in Los Angeles.

It was nearly ten o'clock when she reached the little motel where the cast and crew were staying. "Dreary" was the first word that sprang to mind when she pulled up. A bored-looking night clerk gave her a note that had been left for her from the producer's office and the key to her room, which could only be reached from an outside hallway.

You can tell this commercial is low budget, Ellie thought as she opened the iridescent orange door to her seedy little room and surveyed the cheap floral bedspread, threadbare carpet, and furniture that looked as if it had been picked off the street. *But a job is a job, and my health insurance is now secure.*

She dropped her suitcase, read the note welcoming her to the production, and got ready for bed. After she dove under the flimsy covers, she reached over to turn out the light and realized that the tacky lamp was nailed down to the nightstand. *Talk about putting a fence around a junkyard,* Ellie thought as she closed her eyes.

After a somewhat fretful sleep—always a problem for Ellie the night before a new job—she awoke and was picked up at seven o'clock for the ride over to the set.

"Hi," the twentyish production assistant said to her as he steered the van out of the motel parking lot. To Ellie he looked about twelve. "I'm Bill."

"Hi, Bill," Ellie said. "Isn't anybody else riding with us?"

"The other actors are already over there," he said, then picked up his walkie-talkie, which was squawking every few seconds, to inform somebody at the other end that he had Ellie in the car.

"I understand I'm replacing a vegetarian," Ellie said with a laugh.

Bill rolled his eyes. "She got all the way up here yesterday and then found out it was a commercial for steak sauce. She flipped out."

Ellie frowned. "She didn't know what the commercial was for?"

"She said they told her agent it was for Grandma's tomato sauce."

"Didn't she audition?"

"There were no auditions. The director wanted to save money. It's a fairly new ad agency he's working with, and this is a start-up product. There's not a big budget."

Ellie thought back to the day of the cockroach-spray commercial. It had been done on a shoestring as well.

"So he called actors he had worked with before and hired them. The extras are local people."

"What was the actress's name who quit?" Ellie asked, trying hard not to sound gossipy.

"Lily Wild."

"Lily Wild?" Ellie repeated.

"Lily Wild," Bill assured her.

Ellie was surprised. Lily had been in Ellie's acting class a couple of years before and was notoriously difficult. But she got work in commercials because she was beautiful and the camera loved her. She came across well in reel life, but forget real life. Come to think of it, Ellie mused, she was always munching on a bag of raisins and nuts during the breaks in class and sipping from a bottle of spring water. One of those health nuts who talked about her nutritional intake all the time. Ellie could just picture her freaking out when they told her she'd have to take a bite of steak.

As they drove along, Ellie also pondered the fact that she and Lily were completely different physical types. *I'm surprised I'm her replacement,* Ellie thought.

Ten minutes later they pulled up to a rambling old house, which had been converted into a restaurant, situated on a cliff overlooking the Pacific Ocean.

"How beautiful," Ellie breathed.

"Yeah," Bill agreed. "But I think the place is haunted," he added in an offhand way. He got out of the car and came around to open the door for Ellie.

Inside, people were scurrying about, some with clipboards in hand. Others were at the food table—

the congregating point of any shoot—helping themselves to coffee and grazing on the wide variety of doughnuts and bagels.

Lights were being hung in the big dining room to the left, and a couple of guys were fiddling with the camera. Ellie felt the excitement she always did when she stepped onto a shoot and knew she'd be working. The smell of the greasepaint, the roar of the crowd, she thought. It was steak sauce, not Shakespeare, but it was still show biz. Would she ever be able to get it out of her system and settle into a normal life as her parents so desperately hoped?

Not for the world.

Brad, the director, clad in black jeans, T-shirt, and a baseball cap, hurried over to her. He was thirtyish and hip and had that air of a young Hollywood type on his way up. Ellie noticed that he was also wearing a wedding ring.

"Ellie, it's great to see you," he said, leaning down to give her a kiss on the cheek. "Promise me you're not a vegetarian."

"I eat steak for breakfast," she assured him.

"I love it," he said. "I knew you'd be the one to call. You did such a great job spraying those bugs!"

Ellie laughed. "Remember those hives I got?"

"Do I ever! I'm sorry that commercial never made it to the air. The spray didn't turn out to be the best. It gave you hives but it didn't kill the cockroaches. Just made them lie down for a little while, but then they sprang back to life."

"Little buggers," Ellie said.

Brad put his hand on Ellie's shoulder. "Today you're the chef with the hidden secret. Royalty steak sauce."

"Good enough for a princess," Ellie said. She'd

seen the script. A dining room full of people, including a princess, sit enjoying the chef's secret steak sauce, while the chef is in the kitchen confiding to everyone in TV land that it really came from a bottle.

"You got it. Now let me bring you over to say hello to the people from the ad agency. You've met them. It's the same agency that did the cockroach-spray commercial. They're a little anxious that this sauce be a winner. Then we'll get you into hair, makeup, and wardrobe."

"Great," Ellie said.

Brad was so nice, she thought as she followed him to the food table. Underneath his outward signs of confidence, Ellie suspected there was a certain vulnerability or nervousness. This was his show, and there'd already been problems. Artie had told her that the restaurant had almost backed out of letting them shoot it there. Something about a mixup on the dates.

"Ellie, say hi to Melinda and Robert."

A voice called from the dining room. "Brad, we need you in here!"

"Be right there."

Ellie shook their hands as Brad hurried off. "It's nice to see you again."

"You too," Robert said. He was tall and thin and serious looking. "We're so excited about this commercial. The steak sauce is fabulous."

"Fabulous," Melinda agreed. She was blond and about twenty-five and looked like she could probably be found on Friday nights hanging out at the latest happening club.

"I can't wait to try it," Ellie said. "And I love the script for the commercial."

"Oh, yes," Robert said. "Brad is great. We're so

excited about working with him. The cockroach spray didn't fly, but the commercial was the best. You really came across as hating those bugs, I might add. We loved the commercial *sooo* much that we signed up Brad to do a bunch more for us."

"Um hmmm," Melinda said.

"How wonderful," Ellie declared.

"Fabulous," Melinda said. "Just fabulous."

"Ellie?"

Ellie turned to see a young and pretty dark-haired woman at her side. She was one of the clipboard carriers. "I'm Cassie," she said, with a certain importance. "I'll take you to makeup."

"Go along," Robert urged with a wave of his fingers as he and Melinda wandered off, doughnuts in hand.

"Can I get you a coffee first?" Cassie offered.

"I'd love a cup," Ellie said, then realized that it was not the answer Cassie had wanted to hear.

Armed with her black tote bag and cup of coffee, Ellie followed Cassie upstairs. Halfway up, Cassie stopped on the staircase, turned, and looked down at her. "I'm Brad's wife," she declared menacingly.

"Ohhhh," Ellie said with a big smile, trying her best to be friendly. "When did you guys get married?"

"Two months ago."

"Ohhhh," Ellie found herself saying again. "Congratulations. I noticed Brad's wedding ring and I knew he wasn't married when we did the cockroach commercial six months ago."

"He's married now. We work together."

You mean you work for him, Ellie thought sarcastically. *Boy, does he have his hands full with her.*

Down the hall a bedroom had been cleared out and

set up as a temporary beauty parlor of sorts. A fifty-something actress who was cast to play the princess was sitting in one of the chairs while a makeup artist was busy gluing false eyelashes on her. Ellie recognized her from an industrial film they'd both worked on years before. Samantha Dominoes was a little grouchy and could never get her lines right. "Say it again, Sam," the crew used to quietly joke to each other as the director tore his hair out.

After Ellie had been made up, with her hair styled as reasonably as could be expected under the big chef's hat, she was led to a holding area where she could sit and wait until they were ready for her. The holding area turned out to be a tastefully furnished sitting room down on the first floor that she would share with Samantha and Herb, the actor who would play the prince.

The extras—actors who would be seated at other tables in the restaurant—were together in a big room down the hall.

It was already eleven o'clock and so far there had not been much action. The first scene they wanted to shoot was set in the dining room, where the princess sits at a table with her back to the wonderful view of the Pacific and takes a bite of the steak that has been doctored up with Royal Steak Sauce. On cue, the fog is supposed to roll in in the background as the princess declares, "My darling, this is so much better than what they serve at our drafty old palace."

Samantha was now made up as a princess, with a long ball gown Diana wouldn't have looked at twice and a tiara resting on her teased-up hair. She was sitting on a chair with her feet up, grumbling about the wait. "Where are the phones around here?" she asked Ellie. "There're supposed to be phones nearby. I want to call my agent."

"There's one down the hall," Ellie answered.

"What's taking them so long to get going?" she asked.

"I don't know," Ellie said. "I think it's just the usual 'hurry up and wait.'"

"Aaagghhh!" they heard a woman scream.

Ellie jumped up and went running. There was a commotion outside the picture window, where, through a thick fog, Ellie could make out Cassie standing next to a sparking and sputtering fog machine that looked like it was ready to blow up at any moment.

One of the guys—probably an electrician, Ellie decided—yelled for Cassie to get out of there.

"I was just checking on it," she wailed as flames suddenly shot up from the machine.

"Somebody call the fire department!" Brad yelled. Ellie noticed the terrified expression on his face as he ran outside to comfort his bride.

Robert and Melinda were in the corner shaking their heads. Robert checked his watch. "I'm worried about overtime pay," Ellie heard him grumble to his co-worker.

The fire department arrived within minutes and sprayed down the now charred and blackened fog machine that had seen its last day in show biz.

"What happened to it?" Brad asked one of the firemen after it was all over. His arm was on his wife's back, gently rubbing it.

"Hard to tell just yet," he answered. "Probably a short in it somewhere."

"The place I rented it from assured me it was in good condition," Cassie whined.

"You're just lucky this whole place didn't go up in flames," the fireman said matter-of-factly as he gathered up the hose.

"What are we going to do?" Cassie asked Brad, her brown eyes looking soulfully up into his.

Robert hurried over to them. "Not to worry. The commercial will work better without the fog. We have this beautiful view of the water, so why hide it behind the fog anyway?" He stared intently at Brad. "Let's just get the action going."

Standing nearby, Ellie thought the relief on Brad's face was palpable.

"LUNCHTIME!" someone yelled. "It's time to break for lunch!"

Oh, brother, Ellie thought. Union rules.

Ellie sat in the sitting room with Samantha and Herb and picked at her salad. She wasn't that hungry and didn't know how anybody else could be either. It seemed that all morning everyone was circling the food table, like a bunch of buzzards.

"You two have worked with Brad before?" Ellie asked in an effort to make conversation.

Herb wiped his pencil-thin mustache with his napkin and nodded. He was a man with snow-white hair, an erect carriage, and enough lockjaw to play a prince, Ellie decided. "Lovely fellow," he said. "Very talented. He's really going to go places in this business."

Samantha swallowed a mouthful of pasta salad. "Just as long as that wife of his doesn't get in the way. What a pain in the neck."

"What do you mean?" Ellie asked delicately.

Samantha winced. "She's never been in the business before and now she thinks she's running the

90

show. Bossing everyone around this morning. In the middle of things."

"She tries hard," Herb allowed.

"She's going to ruin it for him," Samantha declared. "She's screwing everything up and is completely jealous of everyone around him."

"Why do you think he lets her be so in charge?" Ellie asked.

Herb looked at Ellie. "My dear, can't you see? He's a man who is madly in love. He wants to make her happy."

After lunch all the actors except Ellie were brought into the dining room, where they were placed at different tables. Samantha and Herb were seated in front of the picture window.

Outside, the crew had a couple of barbecues going, cooking the steaks that would momentarily be placed on the diners' plates. *They could have used the fog machine to cook those steaks,* Ellie thought as she glanced out the window.

In the meantime, Brad rehearsed the lines with Samantha and Herb.

"Now Samantha," he said, "you will take a bite, chew it delicately, swallow, then look at your husband and say, 'My darling, this tastes so much better than what they serve at our drafty old palace. I think we should hire the chef and bring her home. That way we'll find out all her cooking secrets.'"

Samantha cleared her throat, took an imaginary bite of steak, and turned to Herb. "My darling, this is so much better than what they serve at our drafty old home."

"Drafty old *palace,*" Brad interrupted.

"Oh, of course," Samantha said, and she began again. "My dear, this is so—"

"My *darling,*" Brad corrected her.

"Oh, yes. My darling, this is so much better than what they serve at our drafty old palace. We must—uhhh. What are the lines again?"

Ellie escaped into the kitchen. It was too painful to watch, and she could feel the tension building in the room. Melinda and Robert were huddled in the corner, checking their watches. She couldn't blame them. It was afternoon already, and Brad had yet to call "Action!"

Cassie was in the kitchen, supervising the placement of steaks on the plates and the pouring of the sauce over them. To make it easier, the sauce had been placed in a pitcher. Empty bottles of Royal Steak Sauce were in a garbage can nearby.

"Excuse us, Ellie," Cassie ordered brusquely as she and two of the production assistants began to carry the meal into the dining room.

"Of course." Ellie sat down at the big butcher-block table, the empty pitcher in front of her.

Cassie and the others came in and out one more time to grab the rest of the plates.

I'll wait here, Ellie thought. *This is where I'll be working anyway. If they ever get to me. May as well get used to the space. But I'll go get my bag first. It has a magazine I can read.*

After retrieving her bag and peeking into the dining room, where Brad was still rehearsing with Samantha, Ellie sat down again at the kitchen table. Some of the sauce had spilled on it. She put her bag on the chair next to her, pulled out a magazine, and began to read. Within minutes, she began scratching her neck.

92

Oh, please, she thought. *Don't let me start being allergic to something when I'm about to go on camera.* She tried to ignore it, but it kept getting worse. She got up and went over to the sink to splash a little water on her neck, which made it feel a little better.

Just then a production assistant opened the door. He came in to unplug the phone. "We're about ready to roll," he said.

Ellie sat back down and felt herself begin itching even worse than before. Disgusted, she stood up and hurried over to the sink. *Maybe if I wet a paper towel,* she thought. She held it up to the hives that were breaking out on her neck. *This is crazy,* she thought. *The only other time this happened was on that last commercial.*

She hurried over to the table, picked what she thought was her black bag off the floor, and reached in to get out some moisturizer that she always kept on hand and which she thought might help. As she did so, she heard the assistant director yelling, "Quiet on the set!"

This was strange, she thought, feeling around inside the leather tote bag with her right hand as she held the paper towel up to her neck with her left. After a few moments, she put the wet paper towel on the table and looked down. This wasn't her bag she was rifling through! *Oh my God!* she thought, embarrassed at the thought of being seen going through someone else's purse. But what was this familiar-looking shiny can she was holding? She pulled it out. It was an empty can of the infamous cockroach spray! But why? And whose purse was this? She grabbed the wallet and opened it. Tons of credit cards lined up in a row. Cassie's credit cards!

Ellie looked at the spilled steak sauce on the table. With a finger, she took a little taste. It had a rancid flavor. Almost immediately, she could feel angry welts popping out on her neck. Could it be that Cassie . . .

Just as she heard Brad yell "Action!" Ellie burst into the dining room and shouted, "Don't touch those steaks! That's not the right sauce!"

The whole room turned to her in amazement.

Brad, his patience worn thin by the rehearsal with Samantha, tried to keep his tone even. "Ellie, this is not your cue."

"Don't anyone eat the sauce!" Ellie yelled to the actors. "It's been poisoned!"

Robert's and Melinda's eyes looked like they would pop out of their heads.

"What are you talking about?" Cassie demanded. She had hurried to Brad's side.

"You tell me," Ellie said. "What is this cockroach spray doing in your purse? Or, better yet, what is it doing in the steak sauce?"

"There's no spray in the steak sauce," Cassie said, sounding like an angry child.

"Let's have it tested then," Ellie offered.

Brad looked at Cassie in shock. "Cass," he said gently, shaking his head.

Cassie almost blew up. "It was your idea!" She turned to Ellie and pointed over at Melinda and Robert. "They wouldn't release him from his contract doing these commercials and he's been offered a feature film to go to Africa and direct Alex Wheatley's latest bestselling book. That big thick one!"

"That's not true," Brad protested.

Cassie's eyes flashed fire. "Oh, yes it is. You're the one who said the cockroach spray wouldn't kill anybody. It would just make people sick enough that the shoot would get screwed up and maybe you'd get fired. And you hired the vegetarian. You put the short in the fog machine! I taped our conversations just in case I got caught and you decided to abandon me."

As they stood there and fought in front of the stunned room, Robert slipped out and called the police.

All the big thick steaks were left untouched. They would now serve as evidence. So would the thick fog machine. And the contract to direct the movie version of the thick book.

Ellie drove happily to her cousin's house late that afternoon, anxious to have a nice dinner with her cousin and his family. When she pulled the car into the driveway, the kids came running out to greet her and give her a hug.

Peter came to the door and waved as she ambled up the sidewalk, one child on each side, excitedly grabbing her hands.

"How'd it go?" Peter asked as he put his arms around her.

"I've got another good story." She laughed as he ushered her in and closed the door behind them.

A few days later, Ellie's agent left an excited message on her answering machine.

"Ellie, you're not going to believe this," Artie said. "But have I got a job for you. The Royal Steak Sauce people have rewritten the commercial. They loved the way you burst into the dining room to stop people from eating bad steak sauce. They want to use it in the commercial. They're not going to have you say it's poisoned, just bad. Then you hold up the jar of Royal Steak Sauce that you have recently discovered and blah blah blah."

So it came to pass that the chef Ellie Butternut portrayed became the main character in all the Royal Steak Sauce commercials.

And she didn't have to worry about her Screen Actors Guild health insurance for a long, long time.

Revenge and Rebellion

Nelson DeMille
and
Lauren DeMille

Sarah had again grossly overestimated the amount of time it would take to get downtown, leaving her about half an hour to kill before meeting Ron. The rain was getting heavy, so she headed for the first coffee shop she saw, cutting straight across the wind and through the doorway.

This coffee shop reminded her of the one under her apartment, and indeed every other coffee shop in the city, maybe even the country, or the world. New York had these establishments every few blocks as safe havens in a culinary war zone whose boundaries extended to the shores of Manhattan Island. Going to them was like going to a grumpy relative's house for dinner, where the food may be lousy and the treatment possibly worse, but you knew no one would expect you to pronounce things in French, or display any degree of poise or sophistication. Today, Sarah needed such a place, and here she would brace herself for the nearby trendy Soho joint Ron had in store for them.

Seated at a table, she was given a menu, but knew that she should wait to eat with Ron, though she was starving now. Ron, her college friend and failed suitor, now a successful literary agent, was probably forcing himself at two P.M. to eat this third macrobiotic lunch, for Sarah's sake, when all she wanted to do was chomp into a burger right now. She decided that she should really just get some coffee. Decaf. She was already pretty jumpy. Still, she couldn't resist having *something*. She hadn't eaten all day because she was so nervous. Flipping through the greasy, laminated menu, she was struck by a full-color picture of a juicy steak, and French fries covered with melted cheese. "Platter Royale," it was regally dubbed. She was in awe of so much fat on one plate. Her stomach growled in genuflection. Despite this temptation, she decided against food, and put her menu on the small table, which nearly vanished under the menu's huge proportions. Her waiter eventually came around and stood before her, poised with his pen and pad.

"I'll just have a coffee, decaf, please." Her voice cracked on "coffee." She realized these were the first words she had spoken all day.

Her waiter looked confused, then angry. "Coffee, that's all?" He looked at the gathering crowd of people by the door. The rain had worsened, and they were all waiting anxiously for tables, or a seat at the counter. But didn't she have a right just to have coffee? Of course! Who's to say that all of those people would have that $13.95 Platter Royale, or its equivalent? She was here first, after all, and anyway, who was this man standing before her with his stupid pad and

flame-retardant pants? She would not cave. Her
waiter's dark eyes pierced through her own.

"And a Platter Royale, please."

"How do you want that steak?"

"Rare." Her waiter took the menu and left. What
had she done? Could she revoke her order? What
about not caving? What about lunch with Ron? This
was all subconscious self-sabotage. She knew it. She'd
probably be late at this point, and certainly not
hungry. Stupid! Cowardly and stupid! A different
waiter brought her coffee to her, and it was sloshing
all around the saucer. "Could you tell my . . ." she
began, but the restaurant was loud, and he was gone.
Maybe she would just pick at the platter, and then
she'd still be hungry for lunch later. She *was* starving
after all.

She opened the plastic container of nondairy
creamer and dumped it into her steaming coffee, then,
figuring she'd be consuming enough calories with her
impulsively ordered Platter Royale, stirred in a packet
of Sweet'n Low. She took a sip and mangled her face
at the artificial taste of the aspartame, which she just
remembered was derived from petroleum. She put her
cup down and pushed it away. Staring at it, she felt a
surge of metaphysical doubt. How could decaffein-
ated coffee with both artificial milk and artificial
sugar not beg the question, "What is reality?"

She sighed. Her life was quickly descending into
triviality masquerading as the profundity of a *Seinfeld*
episode. Her only hope lay in what she had entrusted
with Ron. Hope is what propelled her through life—
not any great love or passion for her present situation.
She was a freelance writer, which Sarah likened to
prostitution with less pay and mystique. Today, she

should really have been doing research for her present piece, a story for *Nineties Bride* on common loopholes in prenuptial agreements. She was taking the stance that they were purposely constructed by a network of misogynist lawyers and hinted at the fact that they probably created them to use in their own likely divorces. This position was of dubious truth, but served as her crutch through this land of dry legality. Besides, the tone was likely to please the pseudo-militant feminists on the magazine's staff who talked themselves into believing that marriage was a career obstacle, a conspiracy against professional women. They completely failed to see the irony in their present jobs. But really, what was the difference between them and Sarah except that they had a regular source of income and a career worthy of the fear of its being impeded?

Could Sarah have ever gotten married? Probably, but the marriage would have been a case of settling for someone, rather than affirming a great love. All of her friends, now successfully coupled, had introduced her to every unmarried man they knew, regardless of sexual orientation, Sarah discovered. She liked the gay ones. The others, she had systematically offended or embarrassed. Except for Phillip. She would have married him. When she met him, she was at her best, but she later painfully learned that he took this to be her worst. Perhaps he would at least have the decency to function as Beatrice did to Dante, dying early and serving as a muse. But the last she heard of him, he was healthy and still working out at Gold's Gym.

It was now 1:40. Could she make 2:00?

She couldn't wait for the meeting. This was a welcomed and unaccustomed burst of adrenaline.

Ron was finally going to tell her what he thought about her manuscript—face-to-face. This stack of papers, now in his possession, could very well have been a person—Sarah's child, chock full of love, attention, and herself. What would Ron say about it? How odd life was, she reflected. Ron, her virtual slave in college, for four years shamelessly hinting at them dating, not daring to ask because of his valid fear of rejection. Now he had the upper hand.

And a great job. *Literary agent.*

Her steak arrived with a slam on the table and a breeze from her swiftly escaping waiter.

She looked at the massive meal before her. *Wow.* She speared the steak with her fork and its bloody juice oozed with each saw of her knife through its thickness. She chewed on this pinkish chunk, wildly cheered on by the responsive growls of her stomach. She alternated between the steak and the cheese-covered fries.

Her check was placed on the table, causing her to stop in midchew and mumble, "Thank you," though she hadn't asked for the check. She realized she'd eaten about half of both the steak and fries. *Whoops.* Now it was 1:55. She'd be late. Regretting her descent into her id, she got up from the table and paid the cashier.

Outside the coffee shop, under a clearing sky, she oriented herself toward Houston Street and walked briskly toward it. Should she get a cab? Not after the money she'd been intimidated into spending. Besides, she was almost at Prince Street.

As she hurried across Houston Street, Sarah dreamt of a future literary life down here, in the Village or Soho, wearing dark glasses and taking cabs. Her novel would get her here. And Ron would see that it was published. That would be the definitive affirmation of his love for her, getting her autobiographical novel published. It would not only say, "I love you," but also, "and the world will love you. Together we will release this document of your sensitive life to an undeserving, but certainly appreciative public, who will admire your obsession for detail. You've left nothing out . . .."

And indeed she hadn't. Maybe that was bad. Pangs of doubt assaulted her abdomen as she entered Chloe's. *Keep up your nerve,* was her mantra. *You didn't devote this much time, this much work, this* life *to have it given back to you to use as a doorstop, or to cut up into little squares on which to write shopping lists.* She cringed at the thought of "apples, orange juice, tuna fish" scrawled on the backs of pages on which she had dealt with matters of Art, Death, Love—.

"Sarah?" Ron touched her elbow.

"Ron!"

"Hi. You looked a little lost there."

"I'm sorry I'm late."

"Late? Are you?" He looked at his watch. "I guess I am, too. I just got us a table. I never realize how long it takes to get downtown."

"Oh, me neither." He led her to a table up against a side wall. It was a little too exposed for Sarah's taste, discussing her literary accomplishments and aspirations and all.

Sarah and Ron had seen each other a few times in these several years since graduating from college, and he always looked the same, like a little boy whose mother hadn't yet had a chance to fix his rumpled hair and clothes. His voice, always bordering on hysteria, sounded the same, too.

"Are you sure you're all right? You look—"

"Well, I *am* a little wor—"

A waitress came to give them menus and take a drink order. After a quick scan of the wine list, Ron and Sarah each ordered a glass of the house Chardonnay.

Ron was reading the menu. "You're a little what?"

"I'm a little worried about my book. What you have to say about it."

"Sarah, what I say doesn't really matter. I've told you that already. I'm just an agent. If I don't want to represent the book . . ." he paused, realizing the folly of what he was about to say, "perhaps somebody else will."

"Will you represent it?"

"No." He looked up from the menu. "Are you looking at the menu? I see the waitress coming back."

"I don't see her. I'm not hungry, anyway."

"Oh, come on, Sarah! Don't lose your appetite over this. Not at one of the best restaurants in the city. The lamb is very good."

The thought of it made her ill. The waitress returned.

"Can I take your orders?" she asked, striking a pose with her pen and pad.

"I'll have the plate of cookies, please," Sarah said to the now slightly confused, yet accommodating, waitress.

"I'll have the herbed chicken," Ron said. The waitress took the menus and left with a runway pivot on her heel.

"You always did that in college, Sarah. You grossly

exaggerated defeats and then partook in these minor acts of rebellion." He paused. "Despite what your book says."

"I don't recall acting that way at all. My book is how I see myself."

"Conveniently including a blow-by-blow rebuttal of all erroneous things supposedly said about you."

"That's not quite fair . . ."

"Well, your delusion also carries over to your book. Like the Jon character, for instance. You know, the one who 'loved' you in college, unrequitedly, of course—you can never really prove or disprove that type of love years later—and then went on to become a literary agent to whom you gave your novel. With 'Jon' reading the manuscript, 'Lara' imagines him feeling that he is finally in possession of the woman he loves. He has a catalogue of her every thought, feeling, and desire. Possibly it is a guide book on how to win her. I'm sure that in the epilogue, Jon will undoubtedly take a leap of logic and decide that since he loves her, he must share her by getting this *tome* published, lest society be deprived of this emotional Sears and Roebuck."

Their wine arrived.

"And," he continued, "another correction. I think it is far more likely that the characters 'Stacey,' 'Maura,' and 'Blaire' did not like 'Lara' in college not because they were bitterly jealous of her, but rather because they had never before encountered self-centeredness raised to such monumental heights."

Ron had turned red and looked as if he had spent some time planning that diatribe, but had not actually intended to say it. Sarah was too taken aback to react, except by saying, "That's your interpretation."

Ron threw his hands in the air.

"Perhaps, Ron, I should take it to an agent who doesn't know me. Or my past."

"Okay, but I'll tell you now that I don't think any agent *I* know would take it."

"Why are you so angry?" she managed to say.

"I'm angry because you still haven't been humbled. Sarah, I understand your longing for immortality, but do you have to inflict the reading public with this many years of delusions and neuroses? Who would want to read about it?"

"Obviously you did."

He didn't respond. They sipped their wine in silence awhile. The food came.

Sarah looked at him, then said, "Everything came rushing back as I wrote. It was like . . . unfolding my brain, and inspecting what was there."

"Yes, it did feel like surgery."

She glared at him, but it felt like an insufficient response. "You have killed my child, Ron. The only thing I'll ever love."

"Because it's a replica of yourself! And stop the melodrama, please," he said between bites. "Look, I know a few people who *may* be interested in it. I'll pass it on to them, as a favor, and that's why I'm meeting you in person, really. As a favor."

"How many times have you eaten lunch today?"

"Just this once." He laughed then looked at her for a moment.

It's so obvious he still wants me. But what an ass! How could he not respect her book? She wanted to rise above the whole affair, in a seancelike state, but she had to stand by her book, regardless of Ron's assaults. The book was all she had really. She'd lived her life in preparation for writing it, and she wouldn't have that deemed a waste by Ron, who obviously never got over his attraction to her. He was warming.

First he said no to agenting it, then he offered to show it to another agent, next he'd be begging for it, with a minimal percentage. And making this effort to see her! Over lunch! At Chloe's! There was no reason to give up hope yet. Ron was just being difficult, wanting to get her angry, to scare her. Next, he'd be her savior, saving the day for her and for literature. She would have to be forever grateful, after this obnoxious, typically Ron tactic, but one does anything for one's child. . . .

"Be specific," she said. "About the book."

"It's pretty—" he began, as he chewed.

"Brilliant, original, revolutionary?" she helped.

"Long," he said, swallowing. "Are you with the logging lobby, or something? Do you own Hammermill stock?"

"I've recorded everything that's happened in my mind, that I could be expected to remember."

"And then some, I suppose. You seemed to have had more thoughts than every North American combined. Although, I suppose you'd agree with that."

"That's fair, I guess."

He smiled at her. "God, Sarah, you're so . . . crazy, I miss not seeing you every day."

"Love me, love my novel."

"No." He resumed mangling his chicken, as Sarah ate her ridiculous meal of cookies and wine. He asked her, "Why are you having cookies?"

"I ate before I came here. I had a steak."

"What? Where?"

"At the Union Square Cafe with this enraptured editor from Knopf."

"Ah. I see."

"So I don't need you."

"Good. I don't think I can do much for you." He took a swig of wine.

After a few seconds, she asked him, "So, you don't want to be my agent?"

"Sarah, I can't. Your book is clever, but it doesn't really *say* anything. It's beyond editing. You obviously have some talent, but you're misapplying it."

"Yes, on *Nineties Bride,* and *Women Driving,* and *Country Cottage.*"

"That's too bad, but if you do ever write a novel again, I suggest writing something with an ending."

"Do you understand that this book with an ending would mean that I were dead?"

He didn't answer.

"Or would my untimely demise be a good publicity tactic?" She looked at him.

The waitress returned. "Can I get you anything else? Some dessert, coffee . . ." She turned to Sarah. "Some more cookies?"

"I'll have a coffee," said Ron.

"Me, too. And the rack of lamb." Everyone laughed at Sarah's little joke, including Sarah herself, even though she had just suggested commercializing her death. The waitress spun and left, again as if modeling shoes.

"What were you saying?" Ron asked.

"Never mind. I can't write endings. What right do I have to conclude anything?"

"I bet if you got out of that thick fog you're in, you'd be able to comprehend things that you see and hear, rather than thinking people are out to get you. Or love you, unrequitedly." The waitress brought the coffee.

"The rack of lamb is on its way," she said. They all

chuckled the obligatory chuckle. The waitress did her spin and stride.

Sarah said, "I'll listen to literary criticism, but not criticism of myself."

"Sorry . . . but it does seem to be one and the same subject."

Sarah didn't reply.

He smiled and said, "Maybe you could make your novel into a TV series. It never really has to end. It would just be canceled one day."

"Ron. I am very depressed. If I can't write novels, what will I do? I've geared my life towards reaping my inner harvest, gleaning from the richness of my soul. What was that all for?"

"I don't think you really had writing as an objective, Sarah. Maybe you were shy, an introvert. No little girls or boys wanted to play with you at school. Then, one day, as a defense mechanism, fighting against a world that couldn't understand you, you decided to stay in your head. As a coddled child, it works. There's nothing outside your head much worth worrying about. Who would want to leave it? You probably began keeping an angry little diary, you read the *Bell Jar,* you didn't much leave your bedroom—"

"You're wrong, Ron. I kept a diary, but it was a sad little one. I didn't read the *Bell Jar,* because all of the girls at school who wore their depression as a badge of honor read it, and made quite a show of whipping it out of their Lands End backpacks. I forced myself to leave my bedroom and mingle with my peers, partake in activities. But this isn't the world for me, Ron. I've heeded that clichéd advice and written what I knew. And you've deemed it unfit for human consumption."

Ron didn't speak. He just sipped his coffee and

looked out into the restaurant, nodding at two or three familiar faces.

"You know people here?" Sarah asked.

"A few."

It occurred to her that he was well connected to the world of books and that her novel, in which Jon—Ron—came off looking a little silly, would never see life. He was going to smother her child to protect his own ego and self-image. Worse yet, he was criticizing her creation. It was a mistake showing him the manuscript.

She and Ron walked out onto Prince Street together. She said to him, "I'm redecorating and my apartment's a mess. But to thank you for your time and advice, I want to make you dinner. I have the Chloe's cookbook. Why don't I bring the ingredients to your place?" She added, "For old time's sake," and smiled.

He looked at her and smiled back, glad she wasn't overly upset with him. "Sure. How about Thursday?"

"Thursday is fine."

"Do you want to share a cab?" he asked.

"No, thanks. I have some things to do downtown."

"Okay. See you Thursday. About seven?"

"That's fine." She suggested, "I can collect my manuscript then, so you don't have to mail it."

"Good. It's in my apartment. I read it at home."

She smiled. "Late into the night?"

"It kept me asleep until dawn. Just kidding."

They looked at one another a moment, each perhaps thinking of their shared college days. She felt she had to ask one more time. "What should I do with it, Ron?"

He shrugged. "Offer it for posthumous publication."

"Good idea."

They parted on the sidewalk.

Back in her apartment on West 95th Street, Sarah addressed her word processor and typed:

> Two days after my pleasant and encouraging lunch with Jon, I was shocked to hear of his death by poisoning. Food poisoning. Botulism maybe, or E. Coli. I attended his funeral, of course, and a lot of publishing people were there. After the services, we all went to Jon's favorite restaurant, Chloe's, and everyone got up to say something about him. As someone who knew him since college, I was able to relate some bittersweet memories of the Jon most people didn't know. I took the opportunity to read a few pages of my autobiographical novel which featured Jon.
>
> Afterward, a few editors from some major publishing houses approached me—

Sarah stopped typing and thought a moment. This was about as far as she could go for now. Next week, she'd be able to finish this chapter.

She took the newly purchased Chloe's cookbook from her shopping bag and slowly flipped through the recipes.

The Last Peep

Janet Evanovich

U h-oh," Lula said. "There's something crawling on me. I think it's big and black and ugly. And it's not my boyfriend, you see what I'm saying?"

Lula is a former hooker turned bounty hunter in training. She looks like George Foreman with hair by Shirley Temple, and she has the disposition of a '54 Buick. Lots of power under the hood, headlights the size of basketballs, plus you can hear her coming a mile away.

I don't look at all like George Foreman. I'm more like Wonder Woman with a B cup. I'm the bounty hunter who's training Lula, but the truth is, I'm not exactly the bounty hunter from hell. A year ago, I blackmailed my bail bondsman cousin, Vinnie, into giving me this job, and now I'm going one day at a time, hoping the bad guys are all out of bullets.

"This is your fault," Lula said. "You're the one

wanted to see what was in this dumb-ass cellar. Let's go down those rickety stairs and have a look, you said. Let's see if Sammy the Squirrel is down there. And then *slam* the door got closed and locked, and you drop your dumb flashlight and can't find it, and here we are in dark so thick I can smell it. Here we are standing on a dirt floor with things crawling on us."

"I told you to be careful of the door! I told you to make sure it stayed open!"

"Well, excuse me, Ms. Stephanie Plum," Lula said. "I was concentrating on not breaking my neck on the first step which happens to have a board missing."

"We should feel around for a light switch," I said. "There must be a light switch here someplace."

"I'm not feeling nothing. I'm not putting my hands to places I can't see."

"Then give me your gun. Maybe I can blast the lock off the door."

"I don't have no gun. I'm wearing spandex. I'm making a fashion statement here. I haven't got no room for gun bulges. I thought it was your turn to carry the gun."

"I didn't think I'd need it. I wasn't planning on shooting anyone today."

"Yow!" Lula said. "There's something just dropped on me again, and it's moving. Shit! There's another one. There's things all over me, I'm telling you. I bet they're spiders. I bet this place is filled with spiders."

"Just brush them off," I said. "Spiders won't hurt you."

I could be real brave as long as they weren't dropping on me.

"Ahhhh!" Lula yelled. "I hate spiders. There's nothing I hate more than spiders. Let me out of this place. Where's the door? Where's the freaking door?"

The door was at the top of the stairs, but the door was locked. We'd already tried the door.

"Outta my way," Lula said, somewhere in the blackness. "I'm not staying down here with no spiders."

Stomp, stomp, stomp. I could hear her on the stairs. And then *crash!* There was the sound of splintering wood and hinges popping. And a shaft of light cut through the dark.

I ran up the stairs and angled myself through the broken door.

Lula was spread-eagle on her back, on the floor, breathing heavy. "I don't like spiders," she said. "I got any on me?"

"Don't see any."

In all honesty, I wasn't looking too closely because my attention was diverted to a pile of rags on the other side of the room. We'd done a fast, room by room check of the house, but I hadn't looked under the soiled mattress or kicked around in the clutter. Some filthy blankets had been flung against the far wall, and from this angle I could see fingertips sticking out from under the blankets. I crossed the room in two strides, lifted the top blanket and found Sammy the Squirrel aka Sam Franco. He was dead. And he was naked.

The court wanted him for fleeing a charge of indecent exposure. I wanted him for the apprehension fee which was ten percent of his bond amount. Lula wanted him for her share of my share. And so far as I know that was the extent of Sam's being wanted. He was a societal dropout of the first magnitude.

"Uh-oh," I said to Lula. "Sam's turned up."

Lula opened her eyes and rolled her head to the side. *"Yikes!"* she shrieked, jumping to her feet.

The Squirrel had a hole in the middle of his forehead and a toe tag tied to his Mr. Happy. Someone had printed "Get a life" on the toe tag.

"Looks like ol' Squirrel flashed the wrong person," Lula said. "Someone didn't like him wagging his wonkie around."

Seemed like a high price to pay for wonkie wagging. "He wasn't shot here," I said. "No blood and brains on the floor."

"Yeah, and he's been dead awhile," Lula said. "He's pretty stiff." She took a closer look. "Most of him, anyway."

We were in a broken-down, boarded-up bungalow on Ryker Street in Trenton, New Jersey. The house backed up to the Conrail track and was a block from the old Milped Button Factory. There were scrubby fields on either side of the house and beyond that more abandoned bungalows. Very isolated. Excellent place to dump a body.

Everyone knew Sam lived in the house, and everyone knew he wasn't dangerous. Lula and I hadn't expected complications.

Lula cut her eyes side to side. "All of a sudden, this house is giving me the creeps. I don't like dead guys. I especially don't like them with their head ventilated like this."

There was a rattle at the back door and Lula and I exchanged glances.

"Probably the wind," I said.

"I'd go take a look, but one of us should call the police about the body. It's not that I'm afraid, or anything, it's just I got other things to do."

Unlike Lula, I was perfectly willing to admit I was spooked. No way was I staying there all by myself, waiting to get fitted for one of those toe tags using some innovative attachment process. "I'm sure there's no reason to be alarmed," I said. "But just in case, we'll both call the police."

"No need to panic," Lula said.

"Right. No need."

Then we whirled around almost knocking each other over trying to get out the front door. We scuttled across the yard of hard-packed dirt and weeds, to my black CRX and took off, laying rubber.

I usually carry a cell phone, but today it was home, recharging on my kitchen counter, so we drove around, looking for a place to make a call. I used to have one of those gizmos that let my phone charge in my car, but someone stole it, and I hadn't had a chance to get a replacement. If it had been an emergency I'd have stopped and rapped on a stranger's door, but I didn't think five minutes here or there would matter to Squirrel. All the king's horses and all the king's men weren't going to put Squirrel back together again.

I turned onto State Street, drove two more blocks and found a 7-Eleven with a pay phone. I put the call into police dispatch, identified myself and reported the body. Then Lula and I retraced our route back to the bungalow.

A blue and white was already on the scene. Two uniforms stood beside the car. One was Carl Costanza. I've known Carl for twenty-five years, ever since kindergarten. When Carl was nine he could burp in time to the "Star Spangled Banner." This was an accomplishment I unsuccessfully tried for years to emulate.

Carl gave me his long-suffering cop look. "Let me guess," Carl said. "You were the one who made the call."

"Yep."

"Is this the right house?"

"Yep."

"Well, I don't know how to break this to you . . . but there's no body here."

"It's laying in the living room," Lula said. "You can't miss it. It's a naked body with a big hole in its head."

Carl rocked back on his heels, thumbs stuck in his utility belt. "I went all through the house, and there's no body."

Two hours later, Lula and I were eating french fries and sucking milkshakes in the McDonald's lot just outside center-city.

"I know what I saw, and I saw a dead guy," Lula said. "That Squirrel was dead, dead, dead. Someone came and snatched that body. And it wasn't the polite thing to do either, because that was our body. We found it, and it was ours." She crammed some fries into her mouth. "This whole thing is creeping me out."

I was creeped out, too. But more than that I was slack-jawed and bug-eyed with dumbfounded curiosity. What the hell happened to Squirrel? We'd been gone thirty minutes tops. Why would someone dump a body and then remove it?

"I had plans for my share of the recovery fee," Lula said. "I don't suppose Vinnie's gonna give us the money now that some loser came and took our body."

It seemed unlikely since we hadn't recovered anything.

"You know Squirrel?" Lula asked.

"I went to school with him. He was four years older than me. Stayed back a couple times and finally dropped out in junior high. I've only seen him in passing lately."

"He used to talk to me sometimes when I was on the corner doing my previous profession. Used to ride up on that rickety red bike of his. Bet that bike was a hundred years old."

I'd forgotten about the bike. Most street people never ventured farther than a couple blocks. Because Squirrel had a bike he was able to live in an abandoned house and range far and wide for recreational peeping.

"Do you remember seeing the bike at the house?" I asked Lula.

"Nope. That bike wasn't there. And we walked all over with the cops. We looked in the back and the front, and we looked all through the house."

We both thought about that for a moment.

"Squirrel wasn't a bad person," Lula said, serious-voiced. "Was just that his train stopped a few feet from the station. He liked to watch people. Liked to look in bedroom windows at night. And then one thing would lead to another, and pretty soon Squirrel wouldn't have no clothes on, and sometimes he'd get caught and get his bony white ass hauled off to jail."

Lula was right about Squirrel not being a bad person. He could be damn annoying. And seeing his nose pressed against your window at one in the morning could be scary as hell. But Squirrel wasn't mean, and he wasn't violent. And I didn't like that someone had killed him. And, I also didn't like that I'd lost the body. What were the police going to tell Squirrel's mother? *Someone said they saw your son with a bullet hole in his head, but we can't find him. Sorry.*

"This has gotten ugly," I said to Lula.

"Damn skippy. I'm feeling downright cranky about the whole thing. In fact, the more I think about it, the crankier I'm getting."

I finished my milkshake and stuffed the straw under the lid. "We need to find Sam."

"Not me," Lula said. "I'm not looking for no dead guy. I don't like dead guys."

"I thought you had plans for the recovery money."

"Well, now that I think about it I guess dead guys aren't so bad. At least they don't shoot at you."

Usually, I relied on the bond agreement to provide some leads. In this case it wasn't much help. Squirrel's brother, Bruce, had put up the bond to get Squirrel out of jail. Bruce worked at the pork roll factory and was an okay guy, but I didn't think he knew much more than we did about Squirrel. Squirrel was a brother who lived on the fringe. He was a thirty-four-year-old-man with faulty wiring. A man who related to people through panes of glass. A man who lived in an abandoned house, filled with treasures gleaned from the city's trash cans. A man who kept no calendar to remind him of holiday dinners. Squirrel and Bruce could have lived on different planets for all the interaction they'd had in the last ten years.

Myra Smulinski had filed the indecent exposure charge. I knew Myra, and I knew Squirrel must have made a royal nuisance of himself for Myra to call the police. Myra lives on Roosevelt, in the heart of the burg. And mostly Squirrel is tolerated in the burg. After all, that's where he was born and that's where his family still lives.

The burg is a tight Trenton neighborhood of second- and third-generation Italians, Hungarians and Germans. It's roughly shaped like a piece of pie, and it exists only in the minds of its residents.

Windows are kept clean. Numbers runners never miss mass. And at an early age, men learn to change their own oil in the alleys and single car detached garages that hunker at the back of their lots.

Like Squirrel, I was born in the burg and lived there most of my life. Four years ago, at age twenty-six, I moved into an apartment beyond burg boundaries. Physically I'm at the corner of St. James and Dunworth. Mentally, I suspect I'll always be anchored in the burg. This is an admission that causes my sphincter muscle to tighten in terror that someday I'll turn into my mother.

I shoved the last french fry into my mouth and cranked the engine over. "I think we should visit my grandma Mazur," I told Lula. "If there's anything going through the burg rumor mill about Sam Franco, Grandma Mazur will know."

Grandma Mazur moved in with my parents two years ago when my grandpa went to his final lard-enriched, all-you-can-eat breakfast bar in the sky. Grandma is part of a chain of burg women who make the internet look like chump change when it comes to the information highway.

My mother opened the door to Lula and me. She'd never met Lula, and she was making a good effort not to look dazed at seeing a huge blond-haired black woman wearing brilliant azure eye shadow speckled with silver sparkles, shocking pink spandex shorts and a poison green spandex tank top, standing on her porch. Grandma was jockeying for position beside my mother and wasn't nearly so circumspect.

"Are you a Negro?" Grandma asked Lula. "I didn't know Negroes could have yellow hair."

"Honey, we can have any color hair we damn well

want to have. I've got yellow hair because blondes have more fun."

"Hmm," Grandma said, "maybe I need to make my hair blond. I could use some fun."

My father was in the living room with his nose pressed to the sports section. He mumbled a few words about my grandmother having fun on the moon and sunk lower in his chair.

"I've got a couple big thick steaks for supper," my mother said. "And I made a cake."

"We can't stay," I told my mother. "I just stopped around to see if you'd heard anything about Sammy Franco."

"What about him?" Grandma wanted to know. "Are you looking for him? Is this a case you're on?"

"He got arrested for indecent exposure again and didn't show up for his hearing."

"I knew he got arrested," Grandma said. "Poor Myra didn't have no other choice. She said he was always in her backyard. Said he trampled her marigolds into the ground."

"And that's it? That's all you've heard?"

"Is there more?"

"Sammy's been shot. Someone killed him."

Grandma sucked in air. "No! How terrible!"

My mother made the sign of the cross. My father went very still in his chair.

I told them the whole thing.

"I saw a TV show once on body snatchers," Grandma said. "The reason they wanted the bodies was so they could eat their brains."

"Don't mean to disrespect the dead," Lula said, "but those snatchers wouldn't make much of a meal on ol' Squirrel."

Grandma slid her uppers around some while she

thought. "Maybe it was one of Squirrel's relatives that came and got him. Maybe he's downstairs at Stiva's on one of them grooved tables."

Stiva was the burg undertaker of choice, and his mortuary was the social hub of Grandma's universe. She read the obits like other people read the movie section.

"I suppose that's possible," I said. *Anything* was possible.

"I could check it out for you. I was going to Stiva's anyway. Big doings there tonight. Joe Lojak is laid out. There'll be a crowd on account of Joe was an Elk. I'm going to have to get there early if I want a seat up front. And don't worry about me. I can take care of myself. I'll go prepared, if you know what I mean."

I took Grandma aside. "What do you mean by 'go prepared'?"

"I'll take 'the big boy,'" Grandma whispered. "Just in case."

"No! No 'big boy.' No, no, no!"

My mother gave me an inquiring look, and I lowered my voice.

"No 'big boy,'" I said to Grandma. "I thought you promised to get rid of it."

"I was going to," Grandma said, "but I'm sort of attached."

"What's this discussion about?" my mother wanted to know, fixing her eyes on me. "Your grandmother makes a scene at the funeral parlor, and I'm holding you responsible. Last time the two of you huddled like this she set off an explosion and caused three hundred thousand dollars worth of damage."

"It could have happened to anybody," Grandma said. "It was an accident."

* * *

"Like your granny," Lula said when we were back in the car. "Bet she kicks ass at the funeral parlor. What's the 'big boy'?"

"It's a forty-five long-barrel she picked up at a yard sale."

"That the gun she shot the roast chicken with?"

"No," I said. "She shot the chicken with my thirty-eight."

Lula was looking through the bag of food my mother had sent home with me. "You got two cans of peaches, half a pound of sliced ham, some provolone and a tomato. And it looks like there's some walnuts in the bottom of the bag."

"They're for my hamster, Rex."

"Just like going to the supermarket only you don't have to pay."

"Actually, there's a price."

I turned the corner at Roosevelt and rolled to a stop in front of Myra Smulinski's home. There were six houses on the block, all duplex, all two-story. Each half of a house had its own personality, its own small front yard and rectangular strip of backyard. The backyards bordered a single-lane service road which everyone called an alley. Myra's house was fourth in from Green Street. It was July, and Myra had window boxes filled with begonias sitting on her front porch.

Lula looked at the house. "You think Myra whacked Squirrel?"

Myra was in her late seventies. She had seven grandchildren and a hundred-year-old schnauzer who was mean as a snake. She drove a ten-year-old Buick at a consistent twenty mph, and she was burg renowned for her sour cream pound cake. I didn't think Myra was the one who whacked Squirrel.

"Just thought it'd be useful to talk to her," I said.

Myra answered at the first knock. I wasn't sure word had gotten out about Squirrel being shot, so I simply said I was looking for him.

Myra shook her head. "That Squirrel is a pip. I called the police on him two weeks ago, and he's still coming around trampling my flowers. If you're looking for Squirrel, you've come to the right place."

"Have you actually seen him? Or is it just that the flowers are trampled?"

"I saw him the night I made the phone call. Naked as the day he was born. I heard this noise, so I put the light on the back porch, and there he was . . . shaking hands with the devil. It's a wonder the man isn't blind as a bat the way he was working at that thing."

"Have you seen him recently?"

"I haven't, but Helen Molnar said she saw his bicycle laying in the alley when she came home from bingo the day before yesterday."

"Any of your other neighbors see him?"

"Just Helen. She lives at the end of the block next to Green, and she said his bike was laying at the back of my yard. Don't know why he's singled me out. It isn't like I've got something to see."

"Is his bike still on your property?"

"Nope. The bike disappeared."

"You mind if we look around?"

"Go right ahead. Just try not to make too much noise. Lucille's husband, Walter, next door, worked a double shift last night, and he'll be sleeping. I'm getting ready to go out to the beauty parlor. Need to get a fast set to my hair for tonight. Did you hear about Joe Lojak being laid out at Stiva's? He was an Elk, you know. Gonna have to get there early if I want a good seat."

"Gonna have to muscle Granny for it," Lula whispered behind me.

Lula and I walked the length of the street, turned the corner and started down the alley. Helen and Lou Molnar lived in the end house. The other half of the duplex was occupied by Biggy and Kathy Zaremba and their two little kids. Biggy worked for his father. Zaremba and Sons Moving and Storage. There were four sons and mostly what they stored were hijacked cigarettes and CDs. And mostly what Biggy did was play cards with his brothers in the warehouse on Mitchell Street.

Kathy Zaremba's sister, Lucille, lived three houses down, in the other half of the house occupied by Myra. Lucille worked at the hospital, and her husband, Walter, was a security guard.

When we'd walked the alley in its entirety I made my way back, cutting across yards, snooping into windows. All the houses had a back door with a small stoop. The door opened into the kitchen, and there was a room to the other side of the door which was intended to be a formal dining room, but several people, including Myra, had turned it into a TV room.

Several houses had chain link fencing which delineated the yard. Myra and Lucille had foregone the fencing in favor of a low hedgerow bordered with flowers. It was this hedgerow that Sam had mutilated, probably not able to see it in the dark. Neither Myra's house nor Lucille's house had central air. Both had air conditioners hanging butt-out from upstairs bedroom windows. Both had the downstairs windows open. Myra's stoop was nice and tidy, but Lucille's stoop was cluttered with a bag of kitty litter, a rented carpet shampooer, a sponge mop that had seen better days and a broken lamp which was probably on its way out to the garage.

"A bag of kitty litter and a rug shampooer," Lula said. "I bet Lucille's cat peed on the rug."

As if on cue, a gray cat poked its head out the broken screen door. The cat was immediately pulled back and scooped up by Lucille.

"Hi," she said, seeing us standing there.

"I'm looking for Sam Franco," I said. "I know he hung out here sometimes. Have you seen him lately?"

Lucille stepped outside, leaving the cat in the kitchen. She had a roll of red duct tape and a scissors in her hand. She stood still for a moment . . . thinking, lower lip caught between her teeth. "I saw him the night the police came. Don't think I've seen him since then. Sometimes I'd see him on the street, on his bike. Not since that night though."

"You're not gonna be able to patch that door with tape," Lula said. "You need a new length of screen."

"It's the cat," Lucille says. "Every time I put in a new screen the cat pushes it out."

Lucille had a raised welt in the middle of her forehead that was surrounded by a brand-new bruise. I'd been studiously trying not to stare. Lula, on the other hand, was never lost to the dictates of etiquette.

"Boy, that's a beauty of a bruise you're growing," Lula said. "How'd you get that big goose egg on your head?"

Lucille lightly touched the bump. "Wasn't paying attention and ran into a cabinet. Caught the corner."

Lula and I left Lucille to worry about her door and cut across two more duplexes, bringing us up to Biggy's house. Usually there was a Zaremba Moving and Storage Econoline van parked in the alley. It was missing today, along with Biggy's Ford Explorer.

Kathy was in the kitchen, feeding the toddler cereal. I rapped on the kitchen window, and Kathy jumped in her seat and the spoon flew out of her hand.

"Jeez!" Kathy said, coming to the back door. "You almost scared me half to death."

I'd gone to school with Kathy, but we didn't see each other much anymore. She'd been the prom queen in high school. Lots of auburn hair and a fast smile. The hair was the same, but the smile was forced now and didn't reach her eyes. She was too thin, and her face was too pale, the only color being a smudge of a fading bruise high on her cheekbone. No point to blaming that bruise on a kitchen cabinet. Everyone knew Biggy smacked Kathy around.

"I'm trying to find Sam Franco," I said to Kathy. "I don't suppose you've seen him?"

She shook her head vigorously. "No!" she said. "I haven't seen anyone, and I can't talk now. I'm feeding Timmy here."

"That Kathy person is on the edge," Lula said when we were back at the car. "I guess babies'll do that to you."

Not to mention Biggy.

"Maybe we should talk to Biggy," I said. "Maybe we should mosey over to the warehouse and see if he's seen Sam."

The Zaremba warehouse was on the other side of Broad, down by the river. I drove to Mitchell, found a space at the curb at the end of the block and sat staring at the open bay doors. Open doors meant there was no business being conducted today. That was good. Most likely no one would want to talk to me if the warehouse was filled with stolen toasters.

Lula and I got out of the car and walked to the first bay. I flagged down a man wearing Zaremba coveralls and told him I wanted to talk to Biggy. A moment later, Biggy appeared. Biggy looked like a Polish knockoff of King Kong in clothes.

"I'm looking for Sam Franco," I told Biggy. "I know he spent time on Roosevelt Street. I was wondering if you've seen him recently."

Biggy grinned and jingled change deep in the pockets of his pleated polyester slacks. "I saw your picture in the paper when you and your granny blew up the funeral home. You're that twinkie bounty hunter."

"Twinkie?" Lula said, hand on hip. "Excuse us?"

Biggy swiveled his eyes to Lula. "Who's the fatso?"

"That does it," Lula said to me. "I'm gonna shoot him."

Biggy gave Lula a punch to the shoulder that knocked her a couple feet backward. "You aren't gonna shoot anyone, chubs. We don't allow shooting in this neighborhood. It lowers the property values."

Lula got her footing and leaned into Biggy, nose to nose, lower lip stuck out. "Don't you touch me," Lula said. "I don't like people to touch me. You touch me again, and I'll bust a cap up your ass. See what that does to property values, you bag of monkey slime."

Biggy pushed his shirt aside so we could see the 9mm. Glock stuck in the waistband of his pants. "Draw," Biggy said to Lula. "Let's see what you got."

"Hold it!" I shouted. "This isn't the gunfight at OK Corral!"

"He's just being a smart-ass," Lula said. "It's obvious I don't have no gun. Anybody could see I left my gun at home."

Biggy draped his shirt back over his Glock. "I don't

like people snooping around this warehouse. I find either of you here again, and I'm going to get mad. And bad things happen when I get mad."

I grabbed Lula by the hand and pulled her away from Biggy, back toward the end of the street where the car was parked.

"I don't like him one bit," Lula said, shoe-horning herself into the passenger seat of the CRX. "And if you ask me, I think he did it. I think he shot the Squirrel. He wouldn't think nothing of it. He'd just go *bang* . . . squirrel season."

I did some mental eye rolling and stuck the key in the ignition. I returned to the burg and cruised Roosevelt for several blocks, looking for Squirrel's red bike. I took the corner at Liberty and made my way down Hunt, running parallel to Roosevelt, and kept enlarging the area until there was no more burg left.

"Maybe he wasn't in the burg when he was shot," Lula said. "Squirrel went all over Trenton on that bike."

"Okay," I said, "plan number two. You check the Stark Street neighborhood. I'll go home and make some phone calls."

I was halfway through my list of reliable gossipmongers when Eddy Gazarra called. Gazarra was another cop friend, and he was married to my cousin Shirley the Whiner.

"I heard you're looking for Squirrel," Gazarra said. "Dead or alive."

"You know where he is?"

"The boys just opened up a van on the corner of Wall and Perry. Someone called in a nuisance report. Apparently the van's been sitting there in the sun all afternoon, giving off a bad odor, drawing a thick fog of flies."

"Sam Franco?"

"Yeah. Strapped to a hand truck for easy transport. If you hurry you might still qualify for the recovery money."

I was on my feet and out the door before Eddie had a chance to say good-bye. Recovery of a felon wasn't sufficient grounds for a bondsman to get his bond returned. The bondsman's agent had to be present at the recovery. Considering the bizarre history of this case, I might still get the money back if I hustled.

I screeched to a stop behind a pack of cruisers on Perry Street and hit the ground running. I sorted through a gaggle of cops, looking for a friendly face and felt a wave of relief when I picked out Carl Costanza.

"Long time no see," Carl said. "At least four hours."

"Do you think I'm too late to get credit for the recovery?"

"What, weren't you always here? I was first on the scene, and I could have sworn you were already in place."

"I owe you a beer."

"You owe me a six-pack," Carl said. "And a pizza. Large. Pepperoni."

I glanced at the black lettering on the yellow Econoline. "Zaremba Moving and Storage."

"A clue," Carl said.

"Sort of an obvious clue."

Carl shrugged. "Maybe Biggy didn't think the smell would get bad this fast. Maybe he was waiting for it to get dark to dump the body."

"So you think it was Biggy?"

"It's his personal truck. The one he keeps in the alley behind his house. And he's the sort of hotheaded jerk who'd do something like this. I've been to his house twice this month on domestic violence. Never his wife who calls. She's too scared. Always the neighbor or Lucille, the sister."

I agreed with Carl. Biggy was a hotheaded jerk. Trouble was none of the events made sense. "This is all pretty strange," I said to Carl. "I saw this body in the abandoned house this morning. Why would Biggy take it back and put it in his truck?"

"Second thoughts," Carl said. "Happens all the time. You're in a rush to get rid of the body, so you drop it at the first place comes to mind. Then you get to worrying maybe your fingerprints are on his joystick, so you think the river might be better."

There were two suits from violent crimes in the van with Sam. The medical examiner's pickup arrived and backed in close to the truck. The ME drove a dark blue Ford Ranger with a white cap divided into compartments that reminded me of kennels. The ME got out, stepped onto the van's bumper and hauled himself up.

I sat on the curb and waited while everyone did their thing. By the time I got my body receipt signed, the sun was low in the sky. The medical examiner had placed the time of death around two A.M. Even better, he'd been able to ascertain that Sammy'd been killed with a .45 . . . as the slug had miraculously dropped from Sammy's head when one of the attendants lost his grip on the hand truck holding Sam, and the hand truck crashed to the floor, jarring the bullet loose. At least that's the story they told me.

* * *

I didn't feel like being alone with my thoughts, so I ambled over to my parents' house to mooch leftovers.

"Other women have daughters who work in banks and business offices. I have a daughter who looks for dead people," my mother said, watching me eat. "How did this happen? What am I supposed to say to Marion Weinstein when she asks what my daughter does?"

"Tell her I'm in law enforcement."

"You could get a *good* job if you just put your mind to it. I hear the personal products plant has openings."

Just what I wanted to do . . . spend my days overseeing the boxing machine at the tampon factory.

A car door slammed shut out on the street, and Grandma hustled into the house. "You should have been there! That Stiva knows how to do a viewing, I'm telling you. The place was packed. Joe Lojak looked real good. Nice color to his cheeks. Real natural. He had on a red tie with little brown horse heads on it. And the best part was I beat Myra out for the best seat. She even had her hair done, but I got the seat in the first row next to the widow! I'm telling you, I'm good.

"And everybody was talking about Sam Franco! They found him in Biggy's van. And that isn't all. Mildred Sklar was there, and you know Mildred's boy is a police dispatcher, and Mildred said it just came in that they went out to Biggy's house and found the murder weapon in Biggy's closet. Can you imagine!"

"I'm not surprised," my mother said. "Biggy Zaremba is a hoodlum."

"What about Biggy?" I asked. "Did they arrest Biggy?"

"Nope," Grandma said. "He clean got away."

I called Lula and left a message on her machine. "Found Sam Franco," the message said. "So that's the end of that. Give you the details tomorrow."

After two hours of television at my parents' house I still didn't feel comfortable with the Zaremba thing. Not that it was any of my business. My business was simple. Find the missing person. Deliver him to the court. Solving murders was a whole other ball game, and bounty hunters weren't on that team.

"Well," Grandma said, "guess I'm going to bed. Gotta get my beauty rest."

My father opened his mouth to say something, received a sharp look from my mother, and closed his mouth with a snap. My father, on occasion, had likened my grandmother to a soup chicken, and no one was able to deny the resemblance.

"It's late for me too," I said, pulling myself to my feet.

Late enough for me to act like an idiot and snoop along Roosevelt Street under cover of darkness. Don't ask why I felt compelled to do this. Sometimes it's best not to examine these things too closely.

I waved good-bye to my mother and drove down High Street as if I were going home. After three blocks I turned and doubled back and parked at the corner of Roosevelt and Green. The neighborhood was quiet and very dark. No moon in the sky. Downstairs lights were on in all the houses. The burg was a peeper's paradise at night. No one drew their curtains or pulled their shades. Drawn shades might mean your house wasn't immaculate, and no burg housewife would admit to having a dirty house. With the exception of Biggy's house. Biggy's curtains were always closed. Even now when Biggy wasn't in the house, the shades were drawn from force of habit. Biggy had enemies. There were people who might want to snipe at Biggy while he crushed beer cans on his forehead and watched Tuesday Night Fights. I traveled this street all the time, and I knew Biggy never left himself open for target practice.

If this was the movies there'd be a cop watching the Zaremba house, waiting for Biggy. Since Hollywood was a long way from Trenton, I was on the street alone. Round-the-clock surveillance wasn't in the Trenton cop budget.

I followed the sidewalk to the alley and hung a left. I'd only walked a few feet when a car cruised down Green and pulled to the curb. It was a red Firebird with rap music playing so loud the car seemed to levitate at standstill. The driver cut the music and got out of the car. Lula.

"Hah!" she said. "Knew I'd find you sneaking around here. Could hear on the phone you weren't satisfied."

"Curiosity is a terrible thing."

"Killed the cat," Lula said. "Biggy catches you in his yard it gonna kill you too."

"If Biggy has any sense at all, he's on his way to Mexico."

"Uh-oh," Lula said. "Don't look now, but we have company."

The company was Grandma Mazur. She was hustling across the street, waving at us, her white tennis shoes a beacon in the darkness, a distant streetlight reflecting off the big patent leather purse looped into the crook of her arm. I dreaded to speculate what was in the purse.

"I thought you might be coming here to do investigating," she said. "Thought you might need a hand."

What I needed was a parade permit.

"Bet you snuck out of the house," Lula said to Grandma.

"Was easy," Grandma said. "They don't pay attention to me. All I have to do is say I'm getting a glass of water and then walk out the back door."

"I wanted to go through the alley at night," I said. "I wanted to be out here like Sam. See what he saw."

"Then let's do it," Lula said.

"Yeah," Grandma chirped. "Let's do it."

We strolled forward in silence and stopped when we got to the house owned by Lucille and Walter Kuntz. We moved ten feet into the yard, and we could clearly see Lucille watching TV in the back room. She was dressed in a nightgown, her hair was slicked back, and I guessed she was fresh from the shower.

"Where's her husband?" Grandma wanted to know.

"Works the night shift at the stadium. Security guard. Gets off at twelve. Except last night he worked a double shift and didn't get home until eight in the morning."

We simultaneously swiveled our heads to Myra Smulinski's house when the downstairs lights blinked off.

"Myra goes to bed early," Lula said.

We turned our attention back to Lucille. Lucille stayed up late. Maybe she even fell asleep in front of the television.

"Squirrel wasn't peeping in Myra's windows," Lula finally said. "Nothing to see in Myra's windows. Lots to see in Lucille's."

"Nothing to see in Biggy's windows either," I said. "Biggy keeps his shades drawn. So why did Biggy kill Sam if it wasn't for peeking in his windows?"

"Could be anything," Lula said. "Sam could have seen Biggy unloading a van full of hot blenders."

"Maybe it's something homosexual," Grandma said. "Maybe Sam and Biggy were having an affair. And maybe Biggy wanted to end it, and Sam wouldn't hear of it. And so Biggy shot him."

We both just looked at Grandma.

"I was watching television last week and one of them talk shows was about homosexuals," Grandma said. "I know all about them now. And it turns out they're all over the place. You never know who's gonna pop out of the closet next. Some of those homosexual men even wear ladies' underpants. Must be hard to fit your ding dong into a pair of lace panties. Maybe that's why Biggy is so mean. Maybe his ding dong don't fit."

Sort of like the Grinch whose shoes were too tight.

"I gotta lot of theories," Grandma said. "Old ladies got a lot of time to think about these things."

A car swung into the alley and caught us in its headlights.

"Hope it's not the police," Lula said. "The police give me the hives on account of my previous profession."

"Hope it's not my dumb son-in-law," Grandma said. "He gives me the hives on account of he's such an old fart."

I wasn't nearly so concerned about the hives as I was about my life expectancy. I didn't have a good feeling about the car. Normally a driver would slow at the sight of three women walking in an alley. This car seemed to be accelerating. In fact, this car was flat-out aiming for us!

"Run!" I yelped, spinning Grandma around, pointing her at Myra's back door. "Run for cover!"

"Holy cow!" Lula shouted. "This dumb sonnovabitch is trying to mow us down!"

We scattered in three directions. Grandma, having seen the last of her running days, did a fast shuffle to Myra's side of the house. Lula ran to Lucille's side of the house. And for no reason other than dumb panic, I jumped behind the single garage that belonged to Lucille and her husband and sat at the back edge of their lot.

The car slid to a stop, spraying dirt and gravel, the door flew open, and Biggy lunged out and took off after me.

"You!" he yelled. "You set me up! I heard about the police report. You were the first one at the van. You found that body in the house and then you stole my truck and set me up, you pussy liar! I want to know who paid you to set me up!"

He didn't look like a man who would listen to reason, so I bagged the denial and raced for Roosevelt Street. He caught me with a flying tackle in Lucille's side yard, and we both went down to the ground, cussing and clawing. We rolled around without making much progress for a few seconds, and then I accidentally pushed his gonads into the space normally reserved for his pancreas.

"Ulp," Biggy whispered, releasing his grip on me.

"I didn't set you up!" I told him. "I had nothing to do with it."

He dragged himself to his knees. "This is what happens when I help someone out of a jam. I get goddamn screwed. I didn't even kill that little retard, but I'm going to freaking kill you. I'm going to cut you up into little pieces. I'm going to carve my initials in your tongue."

"Help!" I shrieked. I looked around. No one was

coming to help. So I did what any intelligent person would do. I hauled ass out of there. I was moving so fast when I hit Roosevelt Street my feet were airborne. Biggy was thundering behind me. And in my peripheral vision I saw the Firebird rip around the corner and screech to the curb in front of me.

"Get in!" Lula hollered.

I dove into the backseat and the Firebird rocketed away.

Lula slowed after a block. "He's not handling this murder thing well," she said. "Good thing he's not a woman. He'd never make it through the monthly."

Grandma was in the front seat, holding her purse to her chest. "All them Zarembas are soreheads. The whole lot of them. Bunch of big babies."

"We need to call the police," I said. "Who's got a cell phone?"

"Not me," Lula said. "I don't make that kind of money."

"Not me," Grandma said. "I'm on social security."

I had one, but it was in my car, along with my gun and my pepper spray and my stun gun and my bulletproof vest. And unfortunately, my car was parked back on Roosevelt.

"We're only a block from St. Francis Hospital," I told Lula. "You can drop me off there, and I'll run in and make the call."

"Sounds like a good plan to me," Lula said. "That way if Biggy catches up to you, you're real close to the trauma unit."

Lula stopped for a light at Hamilton. High beams flashed in her rearview mirror, and we all swiveled to look.

"Oh, boy," Lula said. "I think I know this car."

I knew the car too. Ford Explorer with bug lights on the top. Biggy's car.

"You might not want to wait for the light to turn," I suggested to Lula. "You might want to move *now!*"

Lula stomped on the gas, and the Firebird jumped forward. Biggy was less than half a car length away, hunched at the wheel, looking like the antichrist, eyes glittering red, reflecting our taillights.

Lula paused at a cross-street and . . . *wham!* Biggy slammed into the back of the Firebird. I felt my head snap, felt the Firebird accelerate again, away from Biggy.

"Did you see that!" Lula squeaked. "He hit my car! I have six more payments to make on this car."

Grandma had a hand braced against the dash. "You think he did that on purpose?"

Wham! Another jolt from behind.

"He's trying to kill us!" Lula said. "That crazy bastard is trying to kill us!"

Grandma leaned her head out the window and yelled back at Biggy. "You stop hitting us this instant! I'm an old lady. You can't go around whacking an old lady like this! I've got bones like a bird. Another crash and my neck could snap like a dry stick!"

Wham! Biggy didn't care much about old ladies' bones.

"Eeeeee," we all shrieked on impact.

Grandma sucked air. "If that don't beat all!" She fumbled in her purse. "I'll put a stop to this! I'll shoot out his tires. That'll slow him down!" She dragged the big .45 out two-handed, leaned out the window for a second time, and before I could reach her, she squeezed one off. A streetlight exploded and the kick from the gun knocked Grandma off her seat. "Dang," she said. "It looks a lot easier in the movies. Clint Eastwood never has this problem."

Biggy gave us another smack from behind, Lula lost control of the wheel, and the Firebird smashed into a parked car and stalled out.

"Okay, now I'm getting irritated," Lula said. "Now my car don't work at all."

We looked back at Biggy, and we gave a collective gasp when he sprang from his car with a tire iron in his hand and raced toward us.

"*Yow!*" Lula shrieked at Grandma. "Shoot him! Shoot him!"

Grandma examined her gun. "Looks to me like I only had one bullet." She rolled her window up. "Don't worry, he can't get to us in here."

Smash. The back window went out with one swing of the tire iron. *Smash.* Another window. I crouched to the floor, cowering and praying, and making promises to God, and safety glass chunked down on me. I should have listened to my mother, I thought. I should have gotten a job at the tampon factory. Hardly anyone got beaten senseless at the tampon factory. If I worked at the tampon factory I'd be home with my nose stuck in a thick book. A smutty romance with a half-naked man on the cover.

Red light flashed through the shattered windows, and I realized cops were shouting to Biggy to get off the car and drop his weapon. I raised my head and saw Carl Costanza looking in at me. "We've gotta stop meeting like this," he said. "People are gonna talk."

It took about an hour to complete the police report, get Lula's car towed away, and receive assurances that Biggy would be locked up and not let out anytime soon. It was a nice night out, and Lula, Grandma and I were only a couple blocks from my parents' house, so we decided to walk. We took a shortcut through the alley behind Roosevelt and fell quiet when we reached Lucille's backyard. Lucille was still watching TV in her nightgown. We stood there for a few moments, all of us lost in our own thoughts. I was the first to break the silence.

"I think Lucille killed Sam Franco," I said.

Lula smacked the heel of her hand against her forehead. "Unh!"

"I think Lucille woke up on the couch here, in the middle of the night, and saw someone looking in her window. I think she got all flustered and got a gun. Walter was a security guard. He would have had guns in the house. Lucille was alone every night. She would have known where the guns were kept. Maybe she kept one in the TV room . . . just in case. Then I think when she was rushing around to get the gun, Sam came into the house. Easy to do if Lucille only had the screen door closed so the house could cool off. Especially if the screen was already broken from the cat. I read through Sam's priors. He'd broken into a house once before. He said he'd been watching a lady get undressed and suddenly he wanted a soda."

"I could see that," Grandma said.

"Makes perfect sense to me," Lula said.

I agreed. I could see Squirrel doing such a ridiculous thing . . . walking into a house buck naked and asking for a soda. "Next thing you know, Lucille, who isn't in a lucid state of mind and isn't even very good with guns, has somehow managed to drill Sam Franco square in the middle of the forehead. He's stretched out in her den (after knocking her lamp over). He's obviously dead. And even more obviously he's unarmed. Walter is working, so Lucille calls the next person on her list. Kathy. And Kathy sends Biggy over to take charge. Biggy possibly having some experience in gangland body disposal, or at least having watched *Goodfellas* a hundred times, tags a message onto Sam and drives him home to the abandoned house."

"What about the part where we leave and the body disappears," Lula said. "You got that all figured out too?"

"The next morning Biggy goes off to the warehouse, and Kathy and Lucille get together and see the potential for getting rid of Biggy . . . who we all know beats the crap out of Kathy on a regular basis."

"Frame him for the shooting," Lula said.

"Exactly. So they hustle over with the moving van Biggy always keeps in his yard, not knowing two people have already seen Sam in the abandoned house, load Sam onto the hand truck, park him and the van in a place with foot traffic and plant the gun in Biggy's closet. Or maybe they don't even have to plant the gun. Maybe Biggy took the gun home with him."

"I think this is all a load of cockydoody," Lula said.

"I saw something like this in a movie," Grandma said. "On that Turner Classics station. I'm pretty sure it was Abbott and Costello."

"I'll tell you when I got this brainstorm," I said. "It was when Grandma fired off that first shot at Biggy and got knocked off her seat. The first time I fired a forty-five I had it too close to my face and the kick knocked the barrel into my forehead. I still have the scar."

"That little white mark?" Lula took a closer look. "Uh-oh, right in the same spot as Lucille's goose egg."

"*Yes!* And I bet the police can find trace evidence all over Lucille's den."

145

"You mean you think there might be some left after she shampooed her rug?" Lula asked.

I'd been so excited about my brilliant deduction I'd forgotten about the rug shampooer.

"No self-respecting burg housewife would leave brain gunk on her walls and floors," Grandma said. "We keep our houses clean. Not like in some of them other neighborhoods."

This was bizarre but true.

"You think we have to tell the cops about your Lucille idea?" Grandma asked.

"It would be the right thing to do," I said.

"Yeah," Lula said. "And we always do the right thing. On the other hand, Biggy Zaremba is a real jerk. I don't like men who beat up on women."

"And kids."

I could feel Lula stiffen next to me. "He beat on his kids?"

"That's what people tell me."

"A man like that should be locked up."

"You could be wrong about Lucille," Grandma said to me. "You don't have any proof."

That was true. I could be wrong. But I didn't think so. Biggy had gone unglued when he saw me in the alley. And he said things he should have kept to himself. Like, how he'd done someone a favor, and how I'd been the one to transfer Sam from the house to the van. Biggy wasn't clever enough to orchestrate a scene like that for his own benefit. Biggy wasn't the killer. Biggy was an accomplice.

"Not only that, but you go telling the cops this theory about Lucille it's gonna take all the fun out of it for them," Lula said. "Homicide won't get no satisfaction if you don't let them figure this for themselves."

Jeez, I wouldn't want to ruin it for homicide.

Grandma shuffled one foot to the other. "There's all kinds of justice, you know."

"Fuckin' A," Lula said.

I thought justice looked like a real big gorilla. I wasn't in the business of determining justice. I was in the business of enforcing the law. But I had to admit, the thought of Biggy in jail sort of warmed my heart.

"Well, we could go to the police station and tell them Lucille's the one," Grandma said. "Or we could go back to the house and have some homemade chocolate cake."

This caught my attention. I'd forgotten about the cake.

"With vanilla ice cream," Grandma said. "The good kind with all them fat grams." She cut her eyes to me. "And hot fudge sauce to go on top."

Grandma wasn't above delivering a well-placed sucker-punch.

"Suppose homicide doesn't figure it out?" I asked Grandma and Lula.

Grandma took a moment to consider. "I guess if it would make you feel better, we could visit Biggy once in a while in the big house. Bring him some cookies."

"Yeah," Lula said, "or we could chip in for a TV. They let them lifers have TV sets."

"We can't just stand by and let a man spend the rest of his life in prison for a crime he didn't commit!"

"The hell we can't," Lula said.

"And besides," Grandma said, "what about all the crimes he got away with? What about the stuff he stole and the people he beat up? What about evening the score?"

I pressed my lips together. "This isn't hockey."

We all shuffled our feet some more, and a drop of

rain splattered on my bare arm. Then another. And another.

"It's a sign from God," Lula said, tilting her face heavenward, squinting into the rain. "God wants us to forget about all this shit and go eat some cake."

Wonderful. Now God was in on it.

"God's no dummy," Lula said. "He knows chocolate cake helps clear a person's head for making important decisions."

I thought about the bruise on Kathy's face. And then I thought about the way the oldest Zaremba kid always looked scared. And then I thought Lula might be right . . . that I wouldn't want to make a decision without the benefit of chocolate cake. In fact, to ensure that I wasn't making a terrible mistake, it might take me a very, very, very long time to make any decision at all.

Going Under

Linda Fairstein

I had dreamed about getting the gold shield ever since I was a kid. My grandfather's detective badge— gleaming yellow metal framing cobalt blue enamel— had attracted and intrigued me for as long as I could remember. I had obeyed my parents' demand that I finish college, but four days after graduation I joined the rookie class at the New York Police Department's academy, to become a cop.

Promotion from the uniformed ranks to the detective bureau can be a long and hard-fought battle. Some officers seem content to walk a beat for their entire careers, while others take daring risks and perform heroic acts to merit the shift to plainclothes investigations. You can't sit for any exams to get the job, the way you can for administrative posts. And I had no one looking out for me down at Headquarters to push me along the way.

There was nothing I wouldn't do, I had vowed to

151

myself the morning I came on the job, to earn that shield.

"Are you out of your mind? You think I'm gonna volunteer to let some guy molest me when I'm not even conscious?" I looked across the table at Mike Chapman, who was chewing the last bite of his cheeseburger as the waitress slipped the check under his plate.

"Chief of detectives asked for you personally."

"He doesn't have a clue who I am, does he?" At the time, I had been working in uniform for two years, assigned to a patrol car on Manhattan's Upper West Side.

"Not really. But when I told him you'd been moaning all over the station house about your abscessed wisdom tooth, he smiled for the first time in half a year."

I pushed away from the table. A week of evening shifts, four P.M. to midnight, had exhausted me completely and drained me of my normal good humor. I had spent most of this tour handling a domestic dispute in a high-rise on Riverside Drive, trying to determine which of the two intoxicated combatants had wielded the first broomstick. The last thing I needed to find when I got back to the command on West 82nd Street was Chapman, who waited for me while I showered and changed into jeans and a sweater. We had walked to a bar on the corner of Amsterdam Avenue, where I nursed a drink while he made me the offer he knew I couldn't refuse.

"What's the deal, exactly?" I asked.

"Lieutenant Borelli says the chief has promised a promotion to whoever agrees to go undercover on this one. Two weeks from today, you could be a third-grade detective. You wouldn't pass up a shot at *that,* would you?"

Chapman worked in the detective squad at the same precinct. He knew I was hungry to get out of uniform and start doing real investigative work, but he also knew that my chances of doing that any time soon—barring some serendipitous arrest of a notorious serial killer—were slim or none.

"I've got principles, Mike. I just can't see myself saying yes to letting some pervert—"

"No problem, pal," he answered, paying our tab at the bar. "I respect you for that. Sandy Denman's been begging me for the case anyway. She'll be thrilled you don't want to step up to the plate on this one."

"What time tomorrow does Borelli want to see me?" I hated Sandy Denman. She'd been on the job only half as long as I had, but Denman had grabbed the commissioner's attention by talking two jumpers in a suicide pact down off the Brooklyn Bridge. One week before that, she had interrupted a robbery in progress at the back door of City Hall, an hour before the mayor's scheduled press conference on the latest figures confirming reduced crime rates in the Big Apple. I'd be damned if I would let Sandy get the shield before I did. "And exactly what do I have to let this dentist do to me, anyway?"

Three days later, on Tuesday morning, I sat in the reception area of the office of Melvin Trichner, DDS, filling out his patient information form using my real name, Samantha Atwell. When I completed the paperwork, I was ushered into one of the cubicles at the end of a long corridor and invited to sit back in his reclining chair and relax.

"This is an awfully thick book, young lady," Trichner said, grinning at me through his bonded, bleached teeth, as he lifted Poe's *Tales of Mystery and Imagination* from my lap and placed it on the counter behind him. "Do you like the macabre?"

Somehow, I had thought the heavy tome would hold my short denim skirt in place throughout the examination, but I didn't protest when Trichner removed it and leaned in to inspect my mouth. "I love thrillers," I answered, before he spread my jaws, hooked his little round mirror on my tender gum, and peered at the lower left quadrant which had been throbbing madly all week.

My hands gripped the arms of the chair as he poked around at the impacted tooth, and I tried to distract myself by staring at the garish assortment of neon-colored flowers and tropical birds which decorated his Hawaiian-style shirt.

"Yes, that baby has got to come out," Trichner announced, rolling away from me on his four-wheeled stool. "How's Thursday morning?" He picked up my chart and studied it to make sure I had answered all the questions about current medications and physical history.

"I'm terrified about the pain," I murmured to him in my whiniest voice.

"I'll give you some pills to hold you over these couple of days."

"Not that pain. I mean, I'm worried about how much it will hurt when you pull my tooth."

Back came a flash of the phony smile, as he clasped his hand on top of mine and rubbed them together several times. "I'm absolutely painless. Some Valium before the novocaine," Trichner offered, "and you'll have nothing but pleasant dreams. Have you got a friend who can take you home afterward? You'll be a bit woozy for a few hours."

"Yeah," I said. "My boyfriend can do that."

"Great. You just dream about him while I put you under. I promise, it'll be an erotic experience."

"Bingo. That's just the language he used to describe what would happen to each of the other victims. This is a 'go.'" Chapman was pumped as he drove me back to the station house from the dental office on Central Park West and 81st Street.

While Borelli and his men plotted the technical procedures for the video surveillance that would monitor our encounter, I sat in the squad room, reading the case reports on the first three complaints.

Victim number one was a student at Barnard College when she visited Trichner eighteen months earlier. She had awakened from the anesthesia in his office after an extraction, certain that he had been kissing and caressing her. She went straight back to her dorm and told her roommate, who brought the young woman downtown to make a police report. Like most professionals, Trichner benefited from peoples' perceptions that they are unlikely to be criminals. Instead of arresting the dentist, Detective Conrad Sully had asked him if he could think of any reason for his patient's bizarre recollection.

"Of course I can," Trichner said, calmly handing the veteran investigator a brochure that described the sedative he had used. "If you read this, you'll see it cautions that the drug is hallucinogenic. What that means is that sexual fantasies are a frequent side effect when we use it."

Sully took the pamphlet back to his office, called the

student to tell her that she had imagined the entire experience, and closed the case out by writing the word *unfounded* at the end of his report.

When the second witness showed up in the same squad room eight months later, the lieutenant referred her complaint to his expert, Detective Sully. This time he didn't even have to leave his desk. The nineteen-year-old hairdresser, who reported that she woke up with her clothing in disarray and a faint memory of being fondled and kissed, read the literature herself before Sully replaced it in his case folder. She left the precinct believing that she had falsely accused poor Dr. Trichner because of her drug-induced intoxication. Sully's brain was sometimes thicker than his brogue.

Mike Chapman was working with Sully when the third victim walked into the station house the week before last. She was an ingenue who had played in a few television soaps, and had been referred to Trichner by her brother when she needed a root canal.

"This gotta be some kind of wonder drug," Chapman remarked. "No other dentist in town has this problem, but all Melvin's patients are dreaming that he's slobbering over 'em."

The circumstances were unique, and no one in the department had ever investigated a matter like this before. Lieutenant Borelli wanted to explore a way to get evidence against Trichner that couldn't be attacked in a courtroom as the product of a witness's imagination. He took his idea to the chief of detectives for approval.

"Borelli asked the chief if he could send in an undercover policewoman and apply for a court order to conceal a video camera in Trichner's office, both to protect the patient and to secure the evidence," Mike said.

"That's legal?" I asked.

"You'll make history, kid," Chapman said. "First time it's ever been done. The chief had to call the district attorney's office to draft the order. They analogized it to a wiretap. The prosecutor told the judge that an audio bugging device like they use in taps wouldn't do any good in a situation like this. This bum doesn't need to utter a word to these women. You could send a dozen undercover cops in, but they'll be sedated, too. Without a camera, we don't have any way to prove what's going on inside. We don't even know what crime he's committing."

"What makes you think he'll hit on *me?*"

Chapman gave me the once-over. "You're his type, Atwell. Long and lean, dark hair, midtwenties. And a little bit flaky. I'm betting he'll want to touch, Sam."

"What'll you charge him with? I mean, what does he do, exactly?"

"That's the mystery, Sam. Nobody remembers, nobody knows."

I got to the precinct at six A.M. on Thursday. It was a steaming hot summer day, so my tank top shirt and tube skirt looked appropriate to the season, and didn't leave much to the imagination. The tech guys from the department had broken into Trichner's office the night before—a court-authorized burglary—and hidden their camera behind the louvered air-conditioning duct, which was perched conveniently above the dental chair. A video monitor was set up in the basement of the building and wired through to the recording device, so Borelli could supervise the operation from underground. In the bottom of my shoulder bag, a Kel transmitter had been secreted, so that the backup team could hear all of the conversation between Trichner and me, and I could summon them at any moment if I was aware of trouble.

Mike was to accompany me to the office and pose as my boyfriend. The minute Borelli observed any improper conduct while I was sedated, he would beep Chapman immediately so he could race down the hallway, open the door to the examining room, and interrupt Trichner in the act. I had signed on for a little bit of sexual abuse—caressing and kissing at worse—but not for anything more invasive than that.

The Muzak was piping in a soulless orchestral rendition of Diana Ross's "Touch Me in the Morning" when the receptionist waved me into the rear of the office to begin the procedure. Mike was singing the lyrics as he watched me walk away. A routine teeth cleaning appointment makes me tremble under the best of circumstances. My anxiety about the procedure seemed palpable as I entered the narrow corridor to surrender myself to Trichner's wandering hands.

Melvin, as he told me to call him, closed the door of the small room after he entered and flipped on the light switch, unknowingly starting up the camera as he gave it the juice. He chattered with me about my personal life as he scooted around on his stool, setting his tools in place for the extraction. Then he lifted my shirt and put the stethoscope against my chest, announcing to me that I had a good, strong heartbeat.

"Think loving thoughts," Trichner told me, stroking my arm as he wrapped the tourniquet in place before he gave me the injection. "You look nervous—they'll calm you down."

GOING UNDER

The last things I remember before going under were the sound of the Boston Pops segueing into a syrupy version of "Feelings," the sight of a flock of shocking pink flamingos on Trichner's shirt, and the warm whoosh of the sedative as he pumped it into my slender arm.

I was lost in a thick fog. Somewhere, off in the distance, I could hear the scraping noise of the door pulling open along its metal tracking, the sound of a familiar voice, the scuffling of several feet, and the words, "You're under arrest, Doc."

The fog thickened and my head rolled from side to side. Someone lowered the headrest on the dental chair and leaned me backward. My eyes flickered open to a display of the pink flamingos, swaying now against a turquoise landscape that was moving with them in undulating waves. The lids closed again, as I continued fighting the nausea.

The noise was gone, and this time there was only a woman in a nurse's uniform, holding my shoulder back against the chair. When I tried to move she explained that I needed to rest in that position, to increase the supply of oxygen flowing to my brain. I was awake, and conscious only of the intense pain in my jaw.

Lieutenant Borelli insisted that Chapman drive me to Roosevelt Hospital, in order for a physician to draw blood so that we could be certain of what drugs Trichner had administered to me. On the way over there, I asked what had happened while I was under.

"Melvin went right to work extracting your tooth. The moment he finished, he pushed the tray which was holding all the dental equipment out of the way. Then he actually lifted you out of the chair and propped you up against his body, holding you in place by wrapping his legs around you."

"But didn't I do—?"

"Do anything? You were in the twilight zone, pal. You were as limp as a rag doll."

"Do I want to know the rest?"

"He lifted the back of your shirt and unhooked your bra. Then he started to caress you, moving his hands around in front, to touch your breasts."

"Didn't I feel that? Didn't I try to stop him?"

"Are you kidding? It's like necrophilia, Sam, only your body was still warm. No wonder these women can't remember anything. None of them even realized he pulled them out of the chair."

"How could he take the chance that I wouldn't come to in the middle of all this and just start screaming at him?" I asked.

"Not a chance. By standing you up, the oxygen doesn't flow to your brain fast enough. You're not gonna regain consciousness until he settles you back in the proper position. You'd never know what happened, as all these complaints prove."

"How long did you let it go on?"

"The guys beeped me as soon as he started to fondle you. Sexual Abuse in the First Degree. We had our felony—didn't need another thing. When I pulled open the door, he had his hands on your rear end, squeezing it and rubbing himself against you. That's where I stopped him."

"Didn't he say anything when you burst in?"

"Yeah," Mike answered. "Trichner told me he was just trying to resuscitate you. That you had gone into respiratory distress and he was trying to help you breathe. Cool as a cucumber."

"What if the judge believes him?"

"Like the DA said when I called to tell her how it all went down, squeezing the buttocks is *not* a recognized means of resuscitation in the medical community. Let him test it out in the Riker's Island infirmary, Sami. I'll be taking Melvin downtown to his arraignment from here," Chapman told me as he left me in the ER. "Call you later."

The lieutenant had one of the guys drive me home, where I spent the rest of the afternoon napping off the anesthesia, nursing my sore mouth, and calming my fatigued nerves after a sleepless night. I was too drained to bother with a can of soup. When the pain hadn't let up by dinnertime, I spent some time in front of the bathroom mirror, surveying the damage of the excavation.

Mike called me at eight o'clock. "Meet me in an hour at the Palm."

"Let's do it another night. I really don't feel like—"

"Don't be such a wimp, Sami. Bring an ice pack for your jaw and get over there."

The cab let me off in front of the restaurant on Second Avenue. It was a New York classic, with lobsters so big you wouldn't want to meet them in a dark alley and enough beef to give a cardiologist nightmares. I walked inside to meet Chapman, who was sitting at the bar with Sully and the team of detectives who had worked the case.

"I'm buying," Mike said. "The judge just set bail for Trichner at fifty thousand dollars. He told the defense attorney that if the videotape showed that his client's hands were anywhere south of Ms. Atwell's mouth during this dental appointment, he didn't want to hear any argument on the merits of the Peoples' case."

"Why did you have to pick *this* place?" I asked,

massaging my swollen cheek as I tried to ignore the incredible smell of the grilled sirloins, fried onion rings, and hashed browns the waiters kept bringing out of the kitchen to the surrounding tables. "The last thing I want to think about right now is a thick steak."

Mike bit his lip as he realized my problem. "Sorry, I wasn't thinking. We just didn't want any more courthouse quiche. I had a real craving for red meat. C'mon, have a drink."

"I can't do that either. I'm on painkillers, remember?"

"Give her a Shirley Temple, straight up," Chapman told the bartender.

The throbbing in my head was still intense.

"What are you still so crabby about, Sami?" he asked me, as the maitre d' told us our table was ready and we carried our drinks over to sit down for the meal.

"You're not gonna believe what that creep did, Mike. He pulled the wrong tooth." An hour ago, when I had examined myself at home, I had discovered that the tooth that had been giving me all the trouble was still there, surrounded by the inflamed gum. In front of it was a gaping hole, where a perfectly healthy molar had been when I awakened this morning.

"The poor fool was in such a hurry to get his arms around you that his fingers must have slipped a bit, Sami. You thought undercover work would be easy? C'mon, we've got something to take your mind off your discomfort, right, guys?"

In front of my seat was a serving platter with a domed lid over it, like they use in restaurants to keep the food warm when it's being served.

Sully reached across me and lifted the handle. More welcome than the choicest filet, there sat a blue and gold shield, with my name engraved below the most beautiful word in the English language: *detective.*

"Cheers, Sami. Borelli says you'll get the real one next Friday, at the promotion ceremonies. And Trichner, he'll get a new degree, too. DDS—Dentist Desires Sex. I think they call it a conviction, where I come from. You put that pervert out of business for us. Welcome to the squad."

I popped a couple of Tylenols with my soda and sat back in the chair, repeatedly stroking the smooth surface of the shiny badge with my fingers and feeling no pain.

Thick-Headed

Walter Mosley

1.

"... the weather was bad and I was in the mood for a thick steak," Fearless Jones was telling me. I knew by the way he was dragging the story out that something was wrong. Fearless was as strong and brave as they come but he got shy whenever he had to admit a serious mistake. "Really I was just thick-headed. I wasn't tryin' t'be, Paris. I mean I was tryin' t'do right. So after Sick Joe gimme the keys to that car . . ."

"Say what?" I asked. "What kinda business you ever gonna have with Sick Joe?"

"He the one gimme the keys."

"What keys?"

"The keys to Panty's Cadillac."

"Panty Martin?"

"Uh-huh. Sick Joe give me twenty dollars from Panty to deliver his new Caddy out to his house in Villa Vista." Fearless swiveled on his high bar stool to give me his *honest* look.

I could see Central Avenue through the green-tinted window behind him. There were people walking and cars gliding along in the sunny afternoon. Not too many sidewalk talkers though. That was 1951 and most colored people in L.A. were at one of their two, or three, jobs.

The bar was empty except for us.

"Ain't Panty Martin the one who you broke his nose?" I asked.

"Yeah."

"But he send Sick Joe to give you twenty dollars to drive out to his house way out somewhere?"

"Yeah."

"Don't somethin' sound wrong to you about that, Mr. Jones?"

Fearless looked at me, pondering the question.

"Not necessarily," he said at last. "Joe said that Panty said that he was sorry about sayin' all them things about me after I ended the fight that he started anyways."

"Joe said that?" I never really accepted the fact that Fearless didn't get sarcasm.

"Yeah. That's what he said. But there was this thick mornin' fog an' I was hungry so I stopped at that li'l place on Pico. You know the one that that nice Japanese man run."

"What happened, Fearless?" I asked.

"It's like this, Paris," he said. "You remember that time we drove down to Pismo Beach with them girls?"

I sighed and said, "Yeah."

"An' you remember how I got a flat but it was a new used car an' I ain't never checked to see if I had a spare tire?"

"You checked the trunk'a Panty's car?" I was interested then. That was at a time in my life when I

168

was always looking for a way to pay the rent that didn't have me going to a regular job.

"Not right off." Fearless stalled again.

I should have paid for our beers and said that I had to go right then. And I would have bowed out on any other man. I am in no way brave. Trouble never sees me if I see him first. But Fearless was my friend. The only real friend I ever had.

I sipped my lager and he tapped his long fingers on the bar.

Everything about Fearless was long and lean. He didn't look like much, even though he was over six feet, but he could be as tough and mean as a barbed-wire fence. He'd killed enough Germans to get a handshake and a kiss from General Patton.

I saw him kill two San Francisco policemen one night who thought they could still mistreat and brutalize black men after the war. Those policemen had it in mind to kill me.

"The trunk," I said.

"The ignition key didn't fit the trunk. I tried to finesse it but I couldn't. I got down on one knee to see if I could jimmy it without breakin' the lock. I couldn't see how to get into it." He looked up at me then. "But there was this smell."

"A smell?"

"A bad smell."

2.

"I took the car over to Tanya Woods's house," Fearless told me. "She got a garage that she never use."

We took the bus to Florence and walked the rest of

the way to Tanya's house. It was just a rental but Tanya kept it as nice as if she owned it. There were rose bushes with mottled red-and-cream flowers along the white wood fence and fruit-laden lemon bushes on either side of the concrete walkway to her door. The inside of her place was nice too, I remembered. It seems that every girlfriend I ever had Fearless had had before, and after, me.

Fearless was a man that women hankered after. After that they'd spend a couple of days with me— waiting to see if Fearless would return.

Fearless led the way to a small path down the side of the house. This led to a door at the back of the garage.

"I got the big do' locked," he said.

The garage was small and dark. Fearless lit a kerosene lantern and held it up so that I could see the Cadillac. It was dark blue and shiny.

"Why you gotta use that lantern, Fearless?"

"Garage ain't wired, man."

He went right to the trunk and threw it open.

The man inside was dead. He wore a green-and-black uniform. His legs were up against his chest and his head was turned slightly downward. The look on his face wasn't so much surprised as it was bemused. There was a big bloody hole in the breast of his green shirt.

"Reynolds," Fearless said.

I knew who it was. Reynolds Weller. One of the first Negro drivers for Pathways—the big interstate bus company. He had three kids.

"This is what Sick Joe told you to take to Villa Vista?"

Fearless nodded.

"Anybody see you in this car?" I asked.

170

Fearless winced. "Yeah," he said. "You know I drove it all over the place. Give some girls a ride. You know."

"Close that trunk," I said. "Let's get outta here."

Tanya's living room was small and cozy. Fearless took the pink couch. I sat on a pink chair. It was so small that it felt like a child's seat—and I am not a large man.

"What can I do, Paris?" Fearless asked me. "You got brains, man. You read all them books."

"We can't leave it here," I said. "Because Tanya would have to turn you in. We can't just dump the car, because people done seen you in it. We can't do your delivery job . . ." I paused a second. "When were you supposed to deliver this thing, anyway?"

"Yesterday."

"Yesterday? Why you wait till today to tell me about it?"

"When I was gettin' ready to leave, Tanya come home," he said. "You know I never come around 'less I want to go out."

"So?"

"Well I didn't want her to get suspicious, so we went out," Fearless said just as if it were the most natural thing in the world. "But I was upset, so I drank too much. I don't know. I guess I passed out in her bed."

"You in here wit' her while Reynolds was out there?" I massaged my face with both hands. "Okay. Okay. You can't make the delivery 'cause you don't know what Joe an' Panty was up to."

"I know what I cain't do, Paris," he said angrily. "What can I do?"

"You got Sick Joe's address?" I asked.

3.

Sick Joe lived on 112th Street.

They called Joseph Hornsby Sick Joe because he was dying of tuberculosis. Coughing and hacking, he'd been dying for the five years since I had met him; some said that he'd still be dying after the year 2000.

Joe lived in a small house behind 1029. We went past his brown Chrysler in the driveway. No one answered our knock.

We went around the back of the house for a little privacy. Over a small fence and through a window, which I had to break, and we were in Sick Joe's two-room home.

We came in through the bathroom window. It was a room so narrow that a fat man would have had to go elsewhere to relieve himself. The bathroom led to a kitchen. I pulled the shades and turned on the lights.

"You go check out the other room," I told Fearless.

There was a half-fried egg in a pan on the stove. The fire was turned off though. The dishes were in soapy water.

"Paris."

"What."

"Here's another one, man."

Sick Joe reclined in his fold-out sofa bed—dead at last. He was naked and peaceful with two bullet holes in his chest. We didn't find anything interesting in the house. I emptied his wallet of four tens, two fives, and a two-dollar bill. I also took his car keys. I didn't think that the bus was fast enough to get us out of the trouble Fearless had gotten us into.

* * *

THICK-HEADED

Fearless and I sat across the street watching Panty Martin in his office—Willard's barbershop.

Panty was an entrepreneur. He took book and numbers, smuggled anything from stolen cars to drugs, and kept two prostitutes on his payroll to turn tricks when times were lean and to entertain business partners when business was good. The lapels on his brown suede suit were too wide, as was the brim of his hat. His shoes were white and his adolescent facial hair needed a trim.

Panty was no larger than I but people respected him just the same. That respect came because of Bobo Brill. Bobo was over six four. If he weighed three hundred pounds only twenty of that was visible fat—all the rest you saw was muscle. Bobo stood outside of Willard's while Panty stretched in the doorway. Behind him Willard and another barber sat in their chairs reading their newspapers.

Panty's girls were in the customer chairs gabbing gaily. Crystal was a dark-colored small-featured kind of pretty. But Kathleen had the proportions and aura of a fertility goddess. I knew both girls, because like I said, I'm small and not handsome either.

"Wait here," I said to Fearless. "You know Panty liable to go off if he sees you."

I walked over to meet Panty. Bobo got in my way but Panty waved him off.

"Paris Minton," he said. His smile held no greeting. "What the hell you want?"

"I need to know sumpin', Panty. Maybe you do too."

"You sound like you need a ass-whippin'," the gangster said.

I tried my best to ignore the threat and walked past him into the barbershop.

Panty and Bobo followed. The barbers and prostitutes looked up at me.

"Hey, Paris," Kathleen said gaily.

"Get up, Amos," Panty said to the young barber. "Let my friend here have a chair."

Amos was maybe ten years younger than I—twenty at most. But he was balding prematurely. His light brown skin shone as if it were waxed. He leapt out of the chair. Crystal stood up as if to protect him but he shied away from her too.

"Take a seat," Panty said.

I did. Bobo moved next to me and I wondered if I should change my address and phone number without giving them to Fearless.

"What can I do for you?" the pimp asked.

"Sick Joe," I said. "Asked Fearless Jones to deliver a blue Cadillac out in Villa Vista for you . . ."

"Let's go," Panty said.

Bobo grabbed my shoulder with a viselike hand. I was lifted out of the chair and thrown toward the back door.

No man or woman in the barbershop raised a voice to prevent my abduction.

We didn't go far. In the alley behind Willard's, Bobo slammed me up against the wall.

"Where my car, Paris?" Panty Martin asked.

"You mean the Caddy?"

Panty slapped like his name but I knew Bobo would get his licks in before long.

"Don't play me, niggah," Panty said. He threw another spaghetti slap and I did my best to pretend that it hurt.

"Man, the car ain't yo' problem."

"Do you wanna get hurt?" Panty asked.

"Listen, Panty," I said. "Fearless got that car from Sick Joe. He found Reynolds Weller in the trunk— dead. Then we went over to Joe's an' he's dead too. Dead. Both of 'em."

I noticed that Panty's dark face was perfectly round, as were his small eyes. The only flaw was a slight bump where Fearless had broken his nose. All that roundness somehow made him seem deficient.

"Where's my car?" he said, proving that he had no imagination whatsoever.

He cared more about his car than he did about death.

"Bobo," Panty said. "Teach this niggah a lesson."

"Hey, Big Bo," Fearless Jones said from behind the men.

As soon as the huge bodyguard took a step away I gave Panty the best breadbasket uppercut of my life. Panty dropped without even a grunt.

Bobo took another step toward Fearless.

Bobo made Fearless look like a twig with a head and hands on it. Even if I had a club I didn't think I could swing it high enough to connect with Bobo's head.

My first impulse was to run.

My second impulse was to run.

With surprising speed Bobo took another step toward Fearless and threw a wild right. That missed but it proved to me that Mr. Jones was dead if left on his own.

I went down on my knees and searched Panty. He had a chrome-and-pearl .25 in his belt.

As I rose with the pistol quivering in my grip Bobo connected with a left to Fearless's jaw. The loud crack was sickening.

I held the pistol with both hands but that only increased the shaking by two.

As Fearless fell, Bobo advanced. But Fearless never hit the ground, at least his body didn't. He put his right hand behind him and literally bounced back up into a fighting stance. Bobo had no chance to realize what was happening. The two roundhouse hooks, left and right, that Fearless delivered to the giant's gut were probably enough, but that swift right uppercut must have broken Bobo's jaw. The bodyguard hit the ground so hard that I thought he had to be dead.

Fearless worried too. He checked the unconscious man's breathing and pulse. Then he came over to Panty. He picked the little gangster up and shoved him against the wall.

"You tell us sumpin', man," Fearless uttered in a chilling monotone. "Or I'm'a kill you for sure."

"What you want?" Panty didn't have any guff left.

"Why you send Sick Joe over to Fearless?" I asked.

"I din't."

"Don't be lyin' t'me now, brother," Fearless warned.

"I swear I din't."

"But when I said about the car," I replied, "you act like you wanted to kill me."

"Somebody stoled my car an' then somebody stoled my money. When you said about the car an' Villa Vista an' Sick Joe I thought it was you. Or maybe you knew about it."

"Joe work for you?"

Panty didn't want to answer but Fearless shook him pretty hard.

"Sometimes," the gangster sobbed. "Sometimes."

Bobo grunted. I looked but he was still out.

"What about Reynolds?" I asked.

"I'ont know no Reynolds, man."

Another deep grunt issued from Bobo. There was a lot of pain in his complaint.

"Let's go," I said to Fearless.

"You got what you need?" he asked me.

"I got all I'ma get here."

"Okay." Fearless gave Panty a short snapping jab to the nose. The little gangster fell to the ground in pain.

"Two times I break your nose," Fearless said to the prone Panty. "Number three an' I break your neck."

4.

By that time Tanya was already home so we couldn't do anything about Reynolds.

"I'ma go back over to her house to keep her outta that garage," Fearless told me.

"Man, don't you never think about nuthin' but tail?"

"That's not it, Paris," he said. "You know they done kicked me outta my place. That's why I wanted that twenty dollars—so I could get a place."

"What happened to that job you had with the baker?"

"Some old customer come in there givin' me lip, that's all," Fearless said.

"You hit him?"

"No. No, I didn't," he said proudly. "But I told him what could happen."

After I dropped Fearless off I went to see what I could see.

Reynolds Weller lived in a small house on Carnation. I didn't know him well. I was taking an adult education class at Jordan High School in bookkeeping and he was studying for the bus driver's test. We'd both smoke cigarettes outside and talk. A couple of times we had drinks with Fearless. But that was all.

The woman who answered the door was obviously holding back her sorrow. Viola Weller was slight and girl-figured even after delivering three raucous boys. Her eyes were as light as brown could get and her skin was the drained color of weathered wood.

"Yes?"

"Hi, Viola," I said.

"Excuse me but I don't recognize you," she said.

"Paris," I said. "Paris Minton. Reynolds told me that he wanted to go bowling sometimes but I lost the number so I thought I'd drop by to make the date."

"I don't know where he is, sir," she replied. "He didn't come home last night."

"Where is he?" I asked, almost believing the concern in my voice.

I noticed then that three small boys, not one older than eight, were standing behind Viola, looking up at me as if hoping that I'd step aside, producing their father from thin air.

"I don't know where he is," Viola said.

"Did you call the police?"

"Police cain't do nuthin' if your man done left you." Viola's voice was dry and hateful.

"You think he's with some woman?"

"You know they cain't he'p comin' by t'tell you about it, mister. Bad news travels on two legs." Viola

178

looked me in the eye then. "You tell'im if you see'im, Mr. Minton, that he got three childrens here. An' if he's wit' her then you tell her that whatever happens it happens again." A shudder went through her neck and Viola Weller closed the door on me.

I drove the dead man's car a few blocks away and parked. The daylight was almost gone but I pulled out my book anyway. The reason I left the Deep South for California was to be able to read. Down there in Texas and Louisiana and Mississippi they didn't encourage black folk to go to the library. The only book they liked you to read was the Bible. All I really wanted was to read. I could have spent my whole life with the *Three Musketeers* and *Oliver Twist, Moby Dick* and the stories of Flannery O'Connor. That day I had found a black writer. *Their Eyes Were Watching God* was in my coat pocket.

I read for a few minutes but I kept seeing Reynolds's death pose. I knew that no book was going to cover that memory; or the smell in Tanya's garage.

I bought a half pint of Seagram's and drove over to a little flophouse on Central named ROOMS 2-3-4. I didn't want to go home because some people knew my address and Panty knew some of them. So I took a second-floor suite for four dollars which meant I got a chair and a blanket. Will Dunne, the proprietor, wasn't happy to see me or my money but it didn't upset him either.

5.

The next morning at about ten I went over to Tanya's, after buying a few pairs of rubber dishwashing gloves.

She was gone, leaving Fearless to lounge around in his boxers.

"You keep her outta the garage?" I asked my friend.

"That's about all," he said. That was the extent of Fearless's bawdy humor.

We donned our gloves and went out to the garage and checked the trunk for money. There was none. Not in the trunk or in the car or under the hood or under the chassis for that matter.

Then we did the worst job: we went through the dead man's pockets. His wallet held his driver's license and three dollars. His other pockets contained fourteen keys on a ring. One of which was a flat, silver O'Keefe with J14 stamped up next to the eye.

It was a gruesome job pulling Reynolds up out of the mess that congealed around him. Fearless did most of the work. Finally we had Reynolds in his new temporary resting place—the trunk of Joe's car.

"What we gonna do now?" Fearless asked.

"*We* ain't gonna do nuthin'," I said. "I'm gonna back the car in the yard back here an' hose out the mess while you go an' take Joe's car somewhere an' leave it."

"An' why cain't you go wit' me?" Fearless asked petulantly.

"Because I didn't take that stupid job, man. Because I didn't get myself into trouble. It's your mess—you go out there an' take the risk."

"Okay," he said. "But where should I take it?"

"Somewhere where there's a lot of black people who drive cars. Somewhere where none'a them black people know your face. And be sure to wipe down the steering wheel and the shift, and all around the doors and dashboard, so your fingerprints ain't on it. An' wear your gloves when you drive it."

180

"Ain't my fingerprints noplace else in the car?" he asked, giving me a look that said he wasn't the only one to make mistakes in that backyard.

"It's only the driver they could prosecute," I said. "Your fingerprints on the passenger's side could just be when you an' Joe went out sometimes."

I spent the morning rinsing blood out of the trunk and off the cement sidewalk into Tanya's small lawn. The smell that Fearless had detected, the smell of death, was still strong after an hour of cleaning. The trunk was attracting flies by the hundreds. The spare tire on the lawn was carpeted with flies. I washed off one half of the tire and then when I turned it over I heard a sound.

The tire was slit along the rim. Inside was a .38 caliber pistol with one shot spent. I thought I knew what that bullet had bought.

After wiping it down as well as I could I drove the Caddy to a free parking lot on Grand Street. Fearless hadn't come back yet but I didn't want to talk to him anyway. I left the .38 under the seat. My duty to my friend was over.

But my troubles were just beginning.

6.

It was the way Will Dunne didn't look at me that got me suspicious. He avoided my nod and greeting just as if I were a white plantation boss.

I went up the flophouse stairs, past the second floor, all the way to the third, and then down the fire escape into the alley.

There was a small soda shop across the street from the hotel. I waited there, half hidden by the booth I sat in, and watched over a cherry Coke.

The two white men, along with Will Dunne, came out in about twenty minutes. Will, who had been tall in his youth, was bent over with age and labor. He held out his big hands in a gesture of confusion. The white men were goons in suits, one blue, the other green. They kept asking Will questions. He kept shaking his head no. After a few minutes of useless discussion the white men got into a black sedan and drove off.

Will watched them go and then spat into the street.

I waited fifteen minutes more before I went over to see him.

Will Dunne was sitting behind his ash desk, a green plastic visor over his forehead. When he looked up there was no emotion on his face. He simply nodded and bit the inside of his cheek.

"I think you owe me a refund, Mr. Dunne," I said.

"I expect so," he replied.

I had Panty's .25 in my hand in my pocket and so I was feeling at ease.

"I gave you twenty," I said. "I think I should have it back."

"I'll give ya sixteen," Dunne said. "You used up four last night."

I pulled the pistol out to give him a look-see.

He took a twenty-dollar bill from his shirt pocket and said, "That's robbery."

"How you gonna blame me for that, old man?" I reached over and plucked the bill from his fingertips. "When you set me up with them hoodlums?"

"That's you, brother," he said. "You the one crossed Mr. Segal."

"Izzy Segal?"

The arthritic hotelier nodded solemnly.

Tanya's number was a Ludlow exchange. I dropped my nickel in a pay phone at a gas station a few blocks from Dunne's.

"Hello."

"Fearless?"

"Hey, Paris. Where are you?"

"You ever hear of Izzy Segal?" I asked.

"Sure. He own all the numbers south'a Crenshaw."

"Well it looks like he got our numbers too."

"What you talkin' 'bout, man?"

I told Fearless about my trouble at Dunne's flophouse.

"It must be sumpin' else, Paris," Fearless told me.

"No, Mr. Jones," I said. "Whatever business it is you messed up, it's Segal's business too."

Fearless was waiting outside of Tanya's house when I got there. He said that she'd be home soon and we wouldn't be able to talk. So we went over to downtown L.A., to McKinley Park. It was late in the afternoon and there were quite a few loiterers like us sitting on park benches around the lake.

"Let's go grab Panty," Fearless was saying. He was quick to take a leadership role when the going got rough. And I had to admit that there was some merit in the idea of going after the man who must've turned us over to the gangster.

But I said, "I'ont think so, Fearless. I'ont think that Panty knows what's goin' on."

"Who in hell care what he knows? He could tell them white men to get off our ass though."

"Panty cain't tell them what to do, man," I said.

"No. Segal wants somethin'. We got to figure out what that is."

"Panty's money?" Fearless offered.

"Maybe. Maybe. But it got to be more than pimp money to get Izzy Segal in it."

"Well, you better find out soon."

"Let's go get some groceries," I replied.

On the south side of the main branch of the Los Angeles library there used to be a ventilation grate. It was heavy but loose. The grate led down to a drainage canal and then up to a door to the subbasement of the library. I was one of the only people that knew about that door or how to get to it. I had spent many a night in the library. There was a nighttime guard but he slept at the big desk near the main entrance and never wandered up to the higher stacks.

"It has to be Reynolds," I said somewhere around midnight.

Fearless was lying flat on one of the study tables. I was in a chair near his head.

"Why you say that?"

"Because he's the piece that doesn't fit," I said. "Look. He's a bus driver and a family man. What's he got to do with gangsters? Nuthin'. He's the key."

I suppose I had to say the words to understand it.

At the First Street bus depot there was a bank of lockers against the west wall, behind a magazine stand so that it was private but not off-limits. The sign over the top of the lockers read PRIVATE. FOR DRIVERS' USE

ONLY. J14 was one of these. Somebody had gotten there before us. The locker had been pried open and then shut. Inside there was a green-and-white-checkered cardigan sweater. In the pocket of the sweater was a solitary photograph of Crystal and Reynolds on a beach somewhere. His big stomach was being caressed by the smiling girl for the camera. Though he was embarrassed by the unflattering pose you could still see that Mr. Weller was deeply in love.

"So that's it," I said in the Bing Cafeteria across the street from the bus depot.

"What?" Fearless asked.

"It was Crystal and Reynolds who did it."

"Did what?"

"Took the money that Panty was holding for Izzy Segal," I said patiently.

"But who killed Reynolds then?"

"I don't know. Maybe it was Crystal or another one'a her boyfriends."

"No," Fearless said with certainty.

"What you mean, no?"

"Crystal wouldn't kill no man for money."

"How do you know?" I asked.

"Believe me, Paris."

"You been wit' her before?" I was amazed that Fearless ever had spent time with a prostitute.

"I know her some—from around. I seen her in the bars an' clubs. She's a sweet girl, Paris." Then he shook his head. "Naw, man. She didn't shoot Reynolds. I don't believe it."

I believed it though. The proof was in the photograph. All I had to do was to get to Panty with that picture and I was home free. Fearless would be too in spite of his doubts.

"Hey, man," Fearless said. "I'm tired. Why'ont we go over to Tanya's an' get some real sleep."

Fearless sleeps like a cat. He said that he didn't want to mess up Tanya's freshly made bed so he curled up on the pink couch, hands and feet dangling idly from every side. He told me that he'd slept in all kinds of bombed-out ruins when he was behind the German lines in the last weeks of World War II.

"Every now an' then I'd hear me a Jerry or two an' I'd get up long enough to go out an' kill'em." I've never understood how such a sensitive and tender man could be so cold-blooded.

7.

When Fearless awoke I had him get on the phone to find an address. Tanya came home soon after that. She was none too pleased that Fearless was entertaining company in her house.

"I don't know who you think is payin' the rent on this place, Fearless Jones," the short, cherry-brown woman said.

"Baby, listen . . ." Fearless began.

"No, you listen," Tanya said.

I remembered her temper and I remembered her heat. I didn't know right then whether I was happy to be out of her sights or not.

"Aw the hell with it! Forget it!" Fearless shouted. "Come on, Paris, let's get outta this woman's house."

He snatched his sweater from the pink couch and took two steps to the door. He pulled the door open and said, "Come on, Paris. I'ont need no woman worry-talkin' me."

I couldn't have followed Paris if I wanted to. Tanya leapt after him. She grabbed his arm and said, "Don't! Don't, baby. I didn't mean to get you upset."

He tried to pull away but it seemed that Tanya was stronger than Bobo when it came to love. She held on for dear life.

I have never understood the kind of hold some men have on women.

It took Fearless a few minutes to be pulled back into the house. He complained that he and I were having problems and that she didn't even care. By the time Fearless had taken a seat Tanya had promised to borrow her sister's car for us to drive while we were settling our difficulties. She even offered to let me sleep on her pink couch.

Anything rather than to see that man leave like that.

I walked the six blocks to Tanya's sister's house while Fearless stayed to comfort Tanya. I knew what was up next for them. Tanya would be happy for a day or two and then she would start to think about how she was humiliated by her man. In a week Tanya would make some impossible demand and then, before he could walk out, she'd kick him out without a backward look.

But that was days away. Right then I had a car. Right then the chances of Fearless and me living to the next week were slim.

Fearless had found that Crystal Craig lived in a big rooming house on Sixty-ninth. She was on the bottom floor in bedroom number six. The front door to the house was open. The sitting room was run-down and threadbare but everything was swept and dusted. There was a stairway to the right. Behind those stairs I found room number six.

She wore a cotton slip with nothing on underneath it. Her small brown eyes registered me but they were too sad to be afraid or upset.

"What you want here, Paris?"

"I brought you somethin'."

"Ain't nuthin' you got that I want," she said. "An' ain't nuthin' in here for you."

I held up the picture of her and Reynolds. She gasped and grabbed for it but I held the photo away.

"Can I come in?"

She backed away and gestured for me to enter just like the girls did in my dreams.

The furnishings of the moll's room were simple. A red desk with a yellow chair. A shelf with pictures of handsome colored men with straightened hair, lightened skin, and razor-thin mustaches. There were also teddy bears and baby dolls on the shelf. She had a single bed that was rumpled. The sheets were clean but deeply marked with the stains of her trade.

"Sit'own," she said.

I took the yellow chair.

"What you want, Paris? You want some pussy for that picture?"

"An' why would it be worth all that to you?"

"I like Reynolds," she said. "I don't want his wife gettin' mad for nuthin'."

I held the picture up to my eyes.

"Don't look like nuthin' t'me," I said.

"You see what you wanna see. I cain't help that." Crystal looked down at her bare knees.

"Reynolds is dead," I said.

She watched her knees for a long time before saying, "I know."

I wondered, and worried, for the first time about Crystal being armed. But it was too late to worry. I

188

should have worried in that bar. I should have worried when Fearless came around to talking about a smell.

"Who killed him, Crystal?"

"I'ont know nuthin'."

"You know Reynolds is dead," I reasoned. "All I got to do is show this picture to Panty an' he jump off my ass an' onta yo' pretty butt."

It took her a moment more of knee reflection.

"Panty was gettin' a delivery on the Pathways from Frisco. Kathleen was gonna pick it up." Crystal spoke in a small girl's drone. "She did it before. I knew 'cause Kathleen told me everything."

"What was on the bus?"

"Money."

"Say what?"

"Kathleen been fuckin' a dude, a vice president in a bank over on Melrose. Big Bill Baretti up in Frisco got a big load'a queer in. So Panty went to Izzy Segal an' said he could pass it at a good rate, sixty-three cent on'a dollar. All Big Bill had to do was send down the money with eighteen percent for the banker in cash."

"Kathleen told you all that?"

"Sick Joe would pick up the money from Panty. Then he'd do business with the banker. Joe an' me had a reg'lar date on Tuesdays. He said if we could get to the driver Panty would be in too much trouble to think about us."

"But instead the driver got to you," I said.

Crystal gave me a hateful sneer.

"Panty been beatin' on me for three years now. An' Rennie was sweet. He put the money in his locker but somebody broke in an' stoled it," she said. "When Rennie went over to Joe an' told'im Joe went crazy an' kilt'im."

My Uncle LeRoy always told me that the only time a wish was sure to come true was when you made it while a whore was crying.

I made my wish right then.

"And then Panty killed Joe?" I asked.

"I'ont know," she cried. "I guess."

"Lucky he didn't tell on you."

"Uh-huh."

"Who else knew about this?" I asked.

"Why?"

"Because I got to give Panty sumpin'. If it ain't you then it got to be the one who broke in that locker."

"Nobody know. Maybe Joe told somebody."

I doubted that.

"Anybody know about you an' Reynolds?"

"Amos," she whispered. "Amos knew that I was gonna get away with Reynolds. Amos knew it."

"And did he know about the money?"

"Uh-uh. No. He knew that Reynolds was gonna steal sumpin' but he didn't know what. An' he didn't know where Reynolds's locker was anyways."

"Tell me about Amos," I said.

8.

I knocked on the door still wondering what I'd say to the woman who didn't know that she was a widow. But I didn't have to worry because Amos answered the door. He must've wondered what kind of fool I was flapping around my pants pockets. He must've wondered until I produced Panty's .25.

"Hi, Amos," I said. "I knew it had to be you told Viola. But I didn't think you'd move in too."

He took a step back into the house without me

having to ask. I came in and closed the door behind me.

"Amos," Viola Weller called. She came in through a door on the other side of the small living room. All she wore was a man's white dress shirt.

"Oh," she said when she saw me.

"Oh," she said a little louder when she saw the gun.

"Hi, Viola," I said. Something about her and the small room made me think of Fearless. I was sure that he was laying up in bed with Tanya right at that very moment.

"What do you want?" Viola asked, but there was little surprise in her voice.

"Where the kids?" I asked.

"At school."

"Then let's sit down. Come on, let's be civilized for a change. Let's talk."

Amos sat in a straightback wood chair. Viola sat on the couch.

"Now that's nice now, isn't it?" I said. "I won't take up much of your time. I want tell you a little story, Vi."

She clenched her hands and watched her knees as Tanya had done.

"It's about a young girl who went astray," I said. "A girl who met a man named after women's underwear. A man who liked to beat on women."

Viola moved her shoulders. Rage rippled down to her fingertips.

"Now this girl was really sweet. She even took ugly ducklings like this one here out back to get a little taste of the good life. Shoot. She didn't even charge Amos. Did she? He was in love."

"Hey, man," Amos said. He was about to stand but I stretched my arm out for a good aim.

That settled the barber back in his chair.

"But then this girl had an idea. All she needed was a gangster and a bus driver. They both loved her too. But you know love don't pay the rent. And so they had to go stealin'. They had to go stealin' an' maybe it woulda come out okay. But your boyfriend here, the one who come and told you about Reynolds and Crystal, the one who you give Reynolds's locker number to. Your boyfriend here stoled the money that they stoled and then the gangster murdered your husband. Killed him dead."

Viola flew out of her chair scratching and kicking. There was blood all down Amos's face. I don't think I could have stopped her in time but then again I didn't try to stop her. Amos finally pushed her off and then slapped her pretty hard.

She fell senseless to the floor.

"Okay, Amos," I said then. "That's enough now. Now it's you'n me."

"What you want from me?"

"There was two packages, man," I said. "I'll take the smaller one and you could keep the other."

The question was in Amos's eye.

"I just want compensation, brother. You did the work. You could have the lion's share and then there won't be no fight later on."

The money was in two boxes in the bedroom. The big box had been spilled out on the bed and spread out.

I guess more than trouble travels on two legs.

I took the smaller box under my arm.

"Why you only takin' the small one?" Amos asked again.

"You want me to take it all?"

There was no reply.

"Come on," I said after a moment or two.

"Where we goin'?" he asked.

"I'ma take you home, Amos. You wanna give Viola a little time to realize that you set up her man to die."

Amos took a pillowcase and stuffed all of the money from the big box in and then we left. Viola was on her feet by then but she didn't say a thing.

I bought a car and gave Fearless twelve hundred of the eighteen thousand dollars grease money. Tanya and Fearless and I then drove down to San Diego and took up residence at the Southern Star Motel—right on the beach. Fearless and I wore Bermuda shorts and sat out in the sun all day long. Tanya wore pink pink sunglasses and a nice, tight pink swimsuit that never got wet. She only stayed a few days though because she had to get back to work.

But unemployment has its benefits if you have a little cash to burn. Fearless and I remained at the Southern Star for three weeks.

I bought the *Herald Examiner* every day just to see what was going on back home. On the second week Amos Sitter was arrested, along with Viola, for passing counterfeit twenty-dollar bills. Reynolds's body had been found the week before.

I ended up feeling sorry for Panty. His real name was Benjamin Martin. After questioning Amos they arrested Panty. It was front-page. PROSTITUTION, COUNTERFEITING AND MURDER. The cops somehow put Panty behind the trigger of the .38 they found in his abandoned car. They also found his fingerprints all over Sick Joe's car and Joe's apartment too. I didn't know if Panty had been in Joe's house but I was pretty sure that he hadn't been in the car, at least not driving like the police said.

Willard's barbershop of prostitution was busted.

When I got back to L.A. the cops questioned me. They searched my pockets for queer and asked some pretty hard questions but they didn't care.

9.

Maybe a month later Crystal Craig came to my door.

"Hey, Paris," she said.

I stepped back for the pretty young thing. She was wearing a pale yellow dress under a blue sweater that was one size too small.

Her every move suggested that I take off my pants for inspection. She sat on my fold-out bed and arched back.

"Where you been, Crystal?"

"Out to my aunt and them in Riverside," she said. "I think Amos told the cops about me an' Rennie. If Izzy Segal hear then they gonna be after me."

There was only one of the sweater's four buttons fastened. She popped that.

I moved to sit down next to her.

"I need some money to get outta town, Paris."

"Do I look like a bank to you?"

"What you doin' tonight?" she asked.

I touched a place high on her neck.

The fear of death, I've heard, is a mighty aphrodisiac. The passion Crystal showed me for the next hour or so went a long way to proving that point.

"You know there's two books in limbo, they say." I was running my hand over the dark brown satin of Crystal's thigh. "A little slender one and then a thick book, a million pages long."

194

"Oh," she said softly, feigning sleep. "What they say, them books?"

"The little one is the list of good people—men and women. I only know one man for sure who got his name in that one."

"An' what's in the other one?" she asked.

"It's a list of all the sinners—big and small. I'm there along with Panty and Bobo and Amos. Viola's in there because she went with Amos for the money. Even though I'm sure she did it for Reynolds's kids it was still a sin."

Crystal sat up and leaned toward me. Her breasts didn't seem like much when she was dressed but naked they were splendid. The size of softballs but not too hard; they were dark but the nipples were even darker and swollen too after all the fear-of-death loving.

"Am I in that thick book?" she asked.

"Especially you," I said. "I mean it has to be a sin to shoot a man you just made love to and then go turn off his half-fried egg."

All of her soft supple cooing went silent and hard. I reached in a drawer next to my bed and came out with three hundred dollars for her. She took it and dressed.

At the door she said, "His gun was in the kitchen. He wanted me to make him eggs after he said that he killed Rennie, after he put his business in what I had give to Rennie. It was his fault for sayin' that an' then leavin' a gun out like that."

"Just go on, Crys," I said.

After she left I thought about calling Fearless. But instead I had two shots of vodka and a long night's nap.

Love's Cottage

Nancy Pickard

*O*n August 14, 1914, seven persons were murdered at the home of the architect Frank Lloyd Wright. The story that follows is a fictionalized account of the events preceding that day.

August 4, 1914
Dearest Mama,

Julian and I are nearing our final destination, on the fastest train between Chicago and a city called Madison in the state of Wisconsin. It is so exciting to be starting a new life. I know that once we reach there all will be well. Julian will be happier and I will forget the frightening events of the past.

We will be met by a car in Madison—as if we were swells, or white people!—and driven to our new posts near Spring Green which is said to be

199

a farming community. We are already far beyond my imagining. With every mile, I feel deeply the distance between us and our beautiful Barbados. In our new home where nobody knows us, Julian shall be butler and I shall be cook.

Mr. John Vogelsang, who so kindly recommended us to Mr. Wright for employment, has told us that our new employer is a very famous man and that the home in which we shall work is one of the most famous houses in this country. It is called Taliesin.

When I inquired of Mr. Vogelsang about the famous man's wife, he said, "That is none of your concern." I do not see how that can be so—do you, Mama?—unless there is a housekeeper who will give me all of my instructions rather than receiving them directly from Mrs. Wright, herself.

Fortunately, Mr. Vogelsang knows nothing of my dear husband's former troubles, or else I fear we would never have attained these new posts. I know there will not be any problems in this wonderful new place where we will work hard and be content and where Julian will be treated with the respect which a proud man such as he deserves.

Oh, Mama, I dearly wish I could actually write to you this letter instead of merely composing it in my head as the train clacks down the track. But lacking all skill with pen and paper, I shall continue to "write" to you as I always have with these thoughts that my brain composes.

I do so wonder what the house where we will be employed will look like. Will it be a grand mansion, do you suppose, all white with painted columns such as the plantations of Barbados? Or, will it be tall and plain and brick such as many Americans seem to prefer? If our new master is a famous man who built his own famous house do you not agree it is most likely to be beautiful and impressive, indeed?

The fields I see are brown and they look dry and we are warned of the danger of fire. But all the talk of the men here in the Negro train car is of the war that has broken out in Europe. Do you know of it? Oh, Mama, my heart is at war, and it feels wounded as I gaze at my dear husband as he talks with such fierce animation to the other men. Would it be terrible for me to say that I almost wish he could be a soldier so that he might find a target for his inner rage? But what if he were himself killed? I must not think in this way.

I wish you could answer your heart-worried daughter, dear Mama, and assure her that she is anxious for no reason, and that if she simply does her own job well, all will be safe and as calm as the bay where once I walked with you at dawn each morning to pick the shells to sell to the Europeans.

Our train is slowing. I miss you.

Gertrude

August 6, 1914
Dearest Mama,

Oh, what a strange house fate has delivered us to. Never have I seen its like. It is long and low and clings to the hillside like an animal seeking shelter from the wind and rain. The ceilings inside are so low I feel as if I must duck my head, and the furniture is strange and looks as if it would be most uncomfortable to sit upon. There are several buildings, and I get very confused and lost just walking from the kitchen to the storehouse. Still, there are gardens with fountains and statues and many shady spots in which to escape the summer sun.

I fear I will be lonely here, for we are situated in the countryside rather than in the town where I might make friends among the servants in the neighbors' houses. But I have heard there is a church where we may be permitted to stand at the rear and listen if we make no noise, so perhaps we will become acquainted with other Negroes there.

The white housekeeper, who introduced herself to us as Mrs. Borthwick, is very nice and quite beautiful with brown eyes, but Julian says she puts on airs. Instead of dusting and cleaning, she seems to spend most of her time writing letters or reading the thick books that fill the many shelves here. She also dresses far too fine for her position as a housekeeper, Julian says, and I do wonder if she steals clothing from her mistress's closet while Mr. and Mrs. Wright are away traveling. Julian says he saw Mrs. Borthwick going into Mr. and Mrs. Wright's bedroom and opening drawers and taking things out and handling them as if they belonged to her!

Still, she has a warm smile and even if Julian feels it is beneath his dignity to take orders from such a presumptuous woman, I find her to be very easy to get along with. Of course, I don't say this to my husband.

We have met other employees, some who work

in the house, others who work for Mr. Wright in his separate office which Mrs. Borthwick calls his "studio." Is he an artist of some kind, I wonder?

We have not met the master yet. He works during each week in Chicago, returning here only on weekends. When I commented to one of the handymen that such constant traveling must be a terrible strain on his wife, he laughed at me quite rudely and asked if I had fallen recently from a turnip truck!

There is an advantage to writing letters to you in my head, Mama, which is that I can do it while I shell peas!

Gertrude

August 8, 1914
Dearest Mama,

Oh! I have never in my life felt so undone, or so shamed. I hardly dare tell you this. Yesterday we went to the church I told you about and, Mama, the topic of the sermon was our employer! And his housekeeper! Only she is not his housekeeper, Mama, she is his paramour for whom he left his devoted wife of twenty years and their six children, and for whom he built this house. The townspeople call it "Love's Cottage"!

Her name was Mamah Cheney when she was married to Mr. Cheney who is a businessman in Chicago. Now she uses her maiden name since her divorce from poor Mr. Cheney. She abandoned her children to come here to Taliesin to live with the famous man.

Oh, I was shocked to my soul and I could barely raise my eyes to meet the stares of the good and respectable people around us. I wished with all of my heart for a thick fog to descend upon that little church and hide us from all of the others. The preacher called the Great Man and his woman all kinds of terrible names and said they should be sent to the fiery pit to be with their father Satan! My husband has said not a word to me since that service. He goes about his duties like a man made of wood.

But what are we to do?

We are here, working for adulterers, far from anywhere, with no friends and no money, at least not until our first payday. I fear we are cast upon the mercy of Jesus.

Gertrude

August 9

Dearest Mama,

So upset was I yesterday that I failed to tell you that we met the Great Man himself. He is not a large person, but he is a dramatic one. He has black hair going to silver and he wears it combed back from his face and falling down past his collar. He dresses quite oddly, in flowing scarves and bizarre hats which I would have thought no respectable gentleman would wear. Of course, now we know that he is not a gentleman!

He seems very busy all of the time.

The house feels full of laughter and noise and excitement in his presence. Mrs. Borthwick fairly glows now that he is in residence. She even complimented Julian on his "English" dignity and reserve, as she put it. They do not know that it is outrage which makes his posture so stiff, and his every word so clipped and "proper."

I pray that Mr. Wright will treat my proud husband decently and courteously, as a master should treat a butler. The ice delivery man told me the Great Man is famous for being charming as pie one day and rude as a snake the next. I know you would not approve, Mama, of my listening to gossip, but I couldn't help but hear the same man say that he had not been paid by this house in almost three months. I do not understand that. Surely in a household which lives as richly as this one does, there should be no problem about paying tradesmen on time. It must be Mrs. Borthwick's fault. He must entrust her with too much responsibility, Julian says, or else she takes the money and spends it on herself. There are rumors that the Great Man has lost the majority of his clients because of his public adultery, but Julian says that he must be rich anyway to build such a house as this.

I am baking three different kinds of pies . . . plum, apple and cherry . . . from the trees in the orchards. I hope to sweeten up Mr. Wright so that he will show only his charming side to my husband!

Gertrude

August 10
Dear Mama,

The terrible weekend is over. The very worst that could possibly happen did happen, and yet we have survived it, so perhaps all may yet be well.

I believed things could not possibly get any worse after our disastrous and mortifying visit to the church on Sunday, and if Mr. Wright had only left early Monday morning as he usually does, I am told, all might have still been well. But he decided to remain at Taliesin for one more day, and that very evening, as Mr. Wright and Mrs. Borthwick were consuming the thick beefsteaks I had cooked for them, Mr. Wright called out to Julian, "Here! Houseboy! Take this empty platter!" It was not only that he called Julian a houseboy instead of by his proper title of butler, but also the manner in which he did so.

Mrs. Borthwick then complimented Julian, not on his impeccable dinner service, but on how handsome he looked in the white coat which takes me an hour every morning to press for him.

My husband felt shamed and patronized. He appears to me to be still seething from the insults and I fear there will be no sleep for me tonight as I listen to him rant about the sinners who employ us. Perhaps another man would not have been offended either by the term or the personal comment, but Julian is not another man. Nothing slides easily off his back, and he was already in a boiling stew from the humiliation in church. It is a terrible, terrible burden to him now to bear the snickering comments and the smirking glances of tradespeople who come to our door with their deliveries. My husband is a decent, God-fearing man for whom such a situation is not to be borne. But bear it we must, for what alternative have we?

Perhaps we can save our pay and try to find posts in a respectable household somewhere else.

I have to go now, Mama, or my tomato soup will run over.

Gertrude

August 11, 1914
Dearest Mama,

I am so busy I cannot think and cook at the same time. The heat is intolerable and makes us all terribly cranky. At least Mr. Wright built this house to catch the smallest cool breeze there might be, which is a blessing. But it is he who also built the dam which provides our own electricity and the dam is always breaking down and our electricity is always going out! Oh, I am irritable, and Julian is beyond the bearing of the most saintly wife, the way he goes on and on about the indignity and degradation of living in the midst of iniquity. As for me, I wish only for the temperature to drop low enough to keep the milk from curdling in the icebox!

Gertrude

August 12, 1914
Dearest Mama,

I am so busy I have hardly time for a thought to spare beyond cooking three large meals a day for unpredictable numbers of persons. This morning, Mrs. Borthwick stepped into my kitchen to tell me her two children are coming for a visit. She appeared excited and happy at the prospect.

I hardly begin to know how to respond to her. I confess I lower my eyes to her as if in observance of the modesty of my position, but the truth is that I do not know how to look such a woman in the face. And yet, I confess, so kindly is her manner, so simple and straightforward her words and so compelling her voice and gaze that my own glance is almost always pulled upward as if she held a magnet.

She is bewitching, Julian says, a wicked, seducing, child-abandoning man-bewitcher. He commands me speak sparingly to her, obey her with a dignity bordering on insolence, and yet it is not in my weak nature to do so. I look down at the floor with all good intentions, but then her soft manner and good humor (she can be very funny!) drag my reluctant eyes up, and before I can stop myself I am smiling back at her. It is said that she has the same effect on many of the decent townsfolk, who find themselves liking her in spite of the example she sets by her very existence here. She will never win over Julian though, neither she nor the Great Man for whom she has disgraced herself.

Of course, I hate myself for my moral weakness.

If Julian caught me at it . . .

Oh, Mama, would that I could be an innocent babe in your arms!

Gertrude

August 13, 1914
Dearest Mama,

One of the other employees was sent to inform me that we will not be paid on the expected date! No reason was given. He says there never is. Never? Does this happen often, I asked him? He shouted at me then, reminding me that there were valiant men at war even as we spoke and their families were suffering and I, a mere Negro woman, should be grateful that I had a bed and food to eat. But he looked, himself, quite desperate, I thought. Is it the custom everywhere for men to vent their anger on the nearest woman?

I am supposed to inform Julian of this worrisome news. They are cowards to give such a daunting task to a mere woman. Would that I owned a battalion of soldiers to stand behind me as I present this news of our imprisonment. Without funds, we are trapped here in what both the preacher and Julian call the "den of Satan." Pray for your loving daughter.

Gertrude

August 14, 1914
Dearest Mama,

Oh, they are a merry bunch today. Mrs. Borthwick is at the dining table even as I compose this letter to you and she is presiding over a luncheon I have prepared for herself and the two children and two of Mr. Wright's draftsmen and two local handymen about the place. It is so gay with the children here, I love the sound of their running feet and their laughter bouncing off the stone walls. Master John is 13 and little Miss Martha is ten.

I wish I felt as gay. Julian, who kept me awake all night with his ranting, hates having to be a servant to the other employees. But he is doing it, nonetheless.

Oh! My cobbler . . .

It is a little later, Mama, and Julian has just taken plates of my rhubarb cobbler into the dining room. The last five minutes in this kitchen have been among the most terrible of my life. He was so angry when he last entered that I was afraid he would strike me. He seemed to have perceived some kind of slight from someone at the table. I don't know what was said, or who it was who uttered the insult, or if it was merely the manner in which the unfortunate words were said. Or, maybe nothing was said, and it only happened in my husband's fevered imagination! I can no longer tell. He sees sin everywhere, too, in the tiniest human error (like missing a single small wrinkle in a sleeve of his white jacket this morning) to the larger offenses of Mr. Wright and Mrs. Borthwick.

I am afraid Julian will actually harm the next man whom he perceives to insult him. I am so afraid . . .

Mama, I smell smoke. I must run to see if I have failed properly to extinguish my cooking fires. I love you.

Gertrude

210

LOVE'S COTTAGE

At noon on August 14, 1914, a recently hired house-man, Julian Carleton, served lunch to Mamah Borth-wick and her guests at Taliesin, near Spring Green, Wisconsin. He is reported to have locked them into the dining room without their knowledge, and then to have set Taliesin aflame by lighting fires under the dining room windows. Then he is alleged to have gone back into the house with an axe, to have unlocked the dining room door and to have killed them all as they tried to escape the fire.

Frank Lloyd Wright was in Chicago having lunch with his son when he received the news of the tragedy.

Julian Carleton was later discovered hiding in the ruins. He is said to have died a suicide, in jail. No motive has ever been established, except for a rumor of his having been slighted by one of the employees who died. Of the fate of his wife, Gertrude, there was no report.

The Road Trip

Ann Rule

Blair Scott was running late as usual; she had meant to be on the road well before six and avoid commuter traffic. This would be her last sales trip by car; another two or three weeks and the brilliance of October would be gone and the passes would be clogged with snow. While the vine maples still blazed scarlet and the larch trees were pure gold, Blair was determined to enjoy autumn—as much as she was capable of joy. As she eased into the flow of northbound traffic on the I-5 freeway, she relaxed a little and pondered for the hundredth, thousandth, time that her world had gradually, insidiously become so full of fear. Blair was running late because she had checked and rechecked all of the new deadbolt locks—even though she knew it was compulsive.

She had married Neil too soon, without a clue that he had a maniacal temper, that he was obsessively jealous. At least she had the guts to leave him, but not without emotional scars. Blair had grown far more afraid in her own house than she ever was on the road. Sensitive, understanding Neil had metamorphosed into an almost-psychotic stalker. She knew that he was responsible for the late-night calls and sounds in the night. *He didn't want me when he had me, but now he won't let me go. . . .*

Blair was half an hour from home when she realized she had forgotten her cell phone. "Damn!" she said out loud. She couldn't turn around; she had an appointment for lunch north of Bellingham with a buyer for a major chain. She flipped on the radio. Dr. Joy Brown was waxing sympathetic with some woman caught in a seemingly insoluble dilemma. Blair settled back against the seat. Somehow, other people's problems made her feel better. Obviously, she wasn't the only idiot in the world. Compared to the woman calling in, Blair felt remarkably well-adjusted.

The I-5 freeway north from Seattle was turning out to be easy; all the traffic jams were in the southbound lanes. Blair even felt a little smug as she sailed past the poor commuters who had to fight traffic every day. If she allowed herself to analyze how she really felt, she would have recognized a feeling akin to being let out of jail—liberated from being frightened for three complete days—but she had learned that deep self-analysis led to anxiety.

She was quite sure that Neil wouldn't get up this early to follow her. He would be calling at eight—a call where he never spoke. She recognized even the intake of his breathing. But she would be long gone. Blair hadn't even turned her answering machine on.

No need. Everyone who mattered knew where she was.

Within an hour, Blair was driving past one small town after another. They all looked quainter and safer clothed in their autumn colors. The sun was out, burnishing everything with a bronze glow. Her left arm on the windowsill felt warm and she hitched up the tight skirt of her suit. She laughed aloud at the man on the radio who was whining about how the *three* women he was engaged to had discovered one another.

"Gotcha, Buster," Blair muttered to the radio.

She wasn't aware of the big semi rig until it was just beside her. When the truck driver leaned on his horn and gave her two loud blasts, she jumped and her foot automatically leapt toward the brake pedal. Blair looked up and saw the driver and his passenger give her grins and thumbs-up. Uncharacteristically, she waved back. Only then did she glance down to see that her skirt was around her thighs.

Blair brushed it down to knee-level, but the huge rig kept pace with her—letting her get ahead in the fast lane, and then hugging her bumper until she had to move over. This was not a game she wanted to play. Not on this first precious day of freedom. She couldn't really see the two men; they were no more than one tan muscled arm on the passenger side, two pairs of sunglasses, and two billed baseball caps.

The semi was silver, with an extended, sleep-aboard cab. Squinting, Blair could see a logo on the side: "Zenith Overland" with a lightning bolt in scarlet beneath the words. She forced herself to keep her head steady and avoid looking at the two men in the cab. When she saw the Roadside Rest Stop: 1 Mile sign, she slowed down and stopped trying to outrun them. She drifted off the freeway and pulled into a parking spot near the rest rooms. Families, people with dogs, and retired couples in polished five-wheelers were all around. They all looked so serene, so comfortable in their lives. She had forgotten how to feel that way.

Blair felt foolish now. Her fear response was too finely honed. *I am afraid,* she spoke silently in her mind. *I am afraid of my ex-husband and strange truck drivers and small airplanes and of being alone and of meeting new people and . . .* Her fear was like a chain of magnetized paper clips; old fears connected to new fears. Blair rested her head on the steering wheel, suddenly cool again in the shade of a yellowed maple tree.

"You okay, miss?"

She jumped and felt something catch in her neck. A face with craters that had taken seven decades or more to create was peering down at her. The old man was wearing a captain's hat that said, Grandpa's Retired. Now, Shut Up! on it.

"I'm fine. Resting my eyes."

He looked doubtful but he touched the funny hat and moved on. She got out, locked the car, and headed for the rest room—halfway to convince him she had stopped for that purpose. She bent her head so she could see in the polished metal that served as a mirror. Once Blair had hated her red hair; now she didn't mind it. She brushed a wispy strand off her forehead and stared at her own eyes, slightly distorted in the reflective panel. Either she was really tired or the panel was smudged. She moved an inch. No—she was really tired. The smudges under her eyes moved too. She hadn't truly slept in such a long time. Her hands trembled slightly as she held them under the blow-dryer.

Damn!

Back on the freeway, she felt better. No silver trucks. No ghosts of marriage-past. She kept her black Celica at a steady sixty-five miles per hour, heading north. The freeway plunged and soared and curved at the same time. Each new vista below was brighter with the trees' last hurrahs. Blair felt her heart rate slow, and then the strange little prickling of her nerves that had become a part of her let go and disappeared.

Fear was akin to having a chronic toothache; after a while, it began to seem normal. She had not realized how uptight she'd been until she relaxed. Blair took a deep breath and smelled burning leaves, the good salt smell of the bays to the west, and clear, cool air.

Her lunch meeting went well. The buyer ordered for dozens of outlets in Washington State and in British Columbia too. The woman and Blair laughed as they thumbed through the greeting cards with ribald humor that would never have flown twenty years ago. Blair really enjoyed selling the cards, the gadgets, and the exquisitely beautiful stationery that her firm produced. It was quality merchandise and she sometimes thought of how pleased both senders and receivers must be with the cards and letters they exchanged.

"You going farther north?" her lunch companion asked.

"Nope. Heading east now." Blair folded the sample kit into its neat compartments. "Across the North Cascades and down to Wenatchee."

"Long way round."

"I know. I guess I'm giving myself a little time-out, even though I'm working. A long drive gives you time to think, you know—and I've always wanted to see the dam. If I don't head up now, it will be too late until next year."

"It's a beautiful drive, but try to be off the mountain by dark. In October, the fog can come out of nowhere and surprise you."

"Oh, I will. I'm going straight through. What time is it now?"

"I've got three-thirty. You'll be pushing it—so I won't keep you."

Blair backtracked south for twenty miles and then turned east. She drove past the entrance to the long-closed state mental hospital and thought what a lonely place it must have been. How awful to have those huge gates close behind you.

The highway began to climb in earnest, past crossroads settlements, then isolated houses with vegetable gardens, and finally into forests that crowded close to the road. At Diablo, Blair pulled over at a tourist view site and gazed at the azure blue of the lake far below. It flowed relentlessly, hypnotically, to the top of the dam before it plunged over to become a power source for distant cities.

It was quiet where Blair stood. There was no one around; it was a weekday, past vacation time, and it seemed that she was the only human being on the pass. She turned, finally, and headed back toward her car.

She heard the truck before she saw it, the gnashing of gears, the rumble of the diesel engine. Its silver shell glinted in the late afternoon sun, and Blair felt her heart convulse as she recognized the jagged red lightning bolt.

Then the horn blared and a male voice shouted—something she could not understand. She did not look

220

up until she was sure that the truck was heading away. Again, she saw only an arm—the driver's arm this time—waving. It was a powerful arm with tattoos that she could not decipher at this distance.

Blair felt a chill and goose pimples appeared on her arms. The sun had disappeared in a moment and it seemed that she could already smell the snow that would fall here soon. She forced herself to wait a good ten minutes before she pulled out of the turnout. The silver truck with its driver and passenger should be far ahead.

She switched on the radio, but there was nothing but static; the mountains blocked all signals. Her beeper was silent, and she suspected that too was at least temporarily incapable of receiving messages. She wished, suddenly, that she had her cell phone and then realized that it too would probably be useless in the walls of rock.

Blair was a good driver, and she concentrated on the winding road, aware of the narrow shoulders that fell away through forested inclines to valleys so far below that she could not judge their depth.

She pushed the button that changed the display on the dashboard from the radio numbers to the clock, and saw with some shock that it was after five. She rolled up her window against the icy air just as she saw the sign: Rainy Pass, 4,855 feet. Blair thought she was at the summit, but the Celica's engine lugged down, still climbing. There was another sign: Washington Pass, 5,477 feet. Closed in Winter.

And then, suddenly, without even a hundred feet of warning, Blair was surrounded by fog so thick that she gasped. For a moment, she could still see behind her, but she could see nothing at all in front of her or to either side. And then the white cloud enveloped her car totally. Everything in her screamed to hit her brakes, but she didn't dare do that. Anyone coming along behind would rear-end her car and send them both off the side, plunging down and down and down through the treetops to the base of the mountain. Still, she feared going forward without knowing what might be in front of her.

"Think . . . *think,*" Blair said out loud. "Don't panic. People drive this pass all the time . . ."

As she adjusted to the white blindness, she was able to discern the faint fog line on the right edge of the road, and—then, if only sporadically—the center line. The Celica moved ahead at ten to fifteen miles an hour, Blair's fingers locked to the steering wheel, her back a rigid mass of muscles. Every so often she could see the tops of trees and then they vanished again into the fog.

She almost wished for the sight of the silver truck ahead. She could at least have used its brake lights glowing red to show her she was still on the road. She turned on her headlights, but they hit the fog bank and bounced back, making the cottony stuff even more impenetrable.

Time passed, but she had no idea how much. She was afraid to take her eyes off the road—or, rather, off the lines that kept her from plummeting over the mountain. It seemed that she was heading down, but she couldn't be sure. Silently, she promised herself that if she came to a town, an intersection, a gas station—*anything* but the white on white—she would stop. She would pull off the road and sleep in her car if she had to.

The Celica's radio came on with a crackling sound followed by a country western singer yodeling loud

222

enough to wake the dead. Blair jumped and almost lost her perspiring grip on the steering wheel. Holding tight with her left hand, she reached over with her right to turn the volume down. And then she saw the image in her rearview mirror and that startled her more than the radio.

The truck seemed to have come from nowhere. It was not in front of her; it was behind her—honking, blinking its lights. Blair had no idea what it—*they*—wanted. She could not drive faster, and she could not see to pull over. And then, blessedly, the fog was gone as quickly as it had come. She *was* going down; she could actually see the road and tree trunks ahead.

She pulled off at the first turnout, and the silver truck sailed by, honking. The passenger hit the side of his door with the flat of his hand. Some signal to express their displeasure at her timidity? She had no idea.

The fog was gone, if only for the moment, but the sun was low behind the trees. Blair realized she was never going to make it to Wenatchee before full dark, and she remembered her vow to stop at the first place she saw. Only there *were* no little businesses at the foot of the mountain, no fruit stands, no gas stations. Nothing. As her hands gradually relaxed on the wheel, she felt the urge to urinate. Given the absence of any sign of civilization, she pulled over once more, locked her car, and headed for a copse of trees. She crouched, aware of how exposed she was, and hurriedly emptied her bladder.

And then she saw the truck. It was parked around a curve just ahead—as if the men inside were waiting for her. She doubted if they could see her there in the woods, but she felt a little thrill of fear. Hurriedly, she yanked up her panty hose and pulled down her skirt, running clumsily to her car. Tears stung her eyes as she struggled to get her door unlocked. *Damn. Damn. Damn.* She was afraid again. It wasn't just Neil who was after her. It was everyone.

Her key slid in, the lock turned, she was behind the wheel. But the silver truck was gone.

She saw the lights of the motel/restaurant/gas station before she saw the low-crouching buildings. Frail blinks of a sign that had more burned-out bulbs than lit ones. The crippled sign said, -l's -abin K-mp. Blair didn't care if Bill or Al or "Hell" owned the "Kabin Kamp." It no longer mattered if it had heat or running water. She was determined to check in until the sun came up again.

The cabins were six separate tiny boxes no bigger than eight by ten feet, with cheap shingle siding. As she signed in at the formica counter, Blair glanced at the restaurant; it had three tables and a counter with a half-dozen stools. Oddly, there appeared to be a dance floor off to the side with a warped floor and a jukebox from the forties or fifties.

The owner—who turned out to be "Cal"— cheerfully gave her a skeleton key on a plastic tab and directed her to the fourth cabin behind the office.

The cabin's door stuck at first and then grudgingly creaked open, releasing a rush of moldy-smelling air. There was an iron bedstead with a thin mattress and a rayon spread with runs in it, a cubicle with a toilet and a sink, a picture of Jesus on one wall and an out-of-date calendar on another. The walls were papered in a brick pattern so that, given the smallness of the room, Blair felt as if she would be sleeping inside a chimney. She didn't care. She lugged her sample cases and her bags in and changed into jeans and a sweat-shirt.

She was hungry. Funny. A half hour ago, she had fully expected to die at the bottom of a cliff, and now that she had survived, all her body's demands were back. Blair grabbed the thick paperback book she always kept in her purse—not to read but to keep strangers from starting conversations. If she was going to eat alone in "Cal's Kafe and Klub," at least she wouldn't have to mingle with the clientele.

When Blair stepped outside and locked the door behind her, she saw that the fog had crept back insidiously, curling around her feet and bouncing higher as she walked through it, but it didn't matter now.

When she turned the corner, Blair saw the silver truck. The cab was empty. She was too tired and too hungry to be frightened; actually, she was annoyed more than anything. Why hadn't she noticed the truck parked off to the side when she checked in? It had probably been there all along, crouched in the shad-ows behind a row of tall cedar trees and what ap-peared to be a communal shower building. The rig didn't look so menacing now; the driver and his side man were likely to be as hungry as she was—and perhaps as tired.

Maybe it wasn't even the same truck. No. Blair knew it was—even as she detoured to check the side for the red lightning bolt, she knew she would find it.

Considering they had all come to what seemed to Blair to be the end of the earth, the restaurant was surprisingly full. There were two big men sitting in the booth farthest from the door, a tall, thin woman eating alone in the middle booth, and a teenaged boy in a jean jacket and wearing cowboy boots, his face abloom with acne, was sitting on a stool at the counter.

Blair hated eating at counters. She was grateful that one booth was empty. She started to slide into the far side so that she wouldn't have to stare at the assembled diners, but saw that the plastic was ripped, exposing the springs. Reluctantly, she sat down with her back to the door and with a full view of the woman, the big men, and the teenager. She had her book open before she was completely seated. It was dog-eared for the first twenty pages, but the seven hundred pages after that were untouched. She had no idea what it was about. She always chose something noncontroversial, nonsexual, non-best-selling—so that no one could conceivably want to discuss it with her. This one was called, *Passages to Nowhere.* Even the title discouraged inquiry.

She didn't have to resort to the book yet, however. Cal held out a menu, mounted on a rustic board, with scarred plastic covering the single sheet of options.

As she perused the menu, Blair felt as if she existed in a time warp. The illustrations were old-fashioned; coffee was a nickel a cup. Maybe she *had* gone off the mountain in the fog and been instantly reincarnated as a traveling saleswoman of the early forties.

She wouldn't be faced with too many choices: "Slsbry Stk with Brn Grvy; Trky Pt Pie; Thck Rb-ye Stk, all with Chc. of Pot., Veg. Des. Brd." Apparently Cal had been influenced by his neon sign, and no longer saw a need to spell *anything* out completely. Blair smiled faintly, and the woman in the next booth smiled back. She studied the woman in quick, casual glances around the cafe—and out of the corner of her eye. She could not discern her age; she might have been thirty or forty-five. She wore a dark business suit, and her hair was wrapped in an expensive silk scarf. Her glasses were tinted slightly so that it was difficult to see her eyes. She probably felt as out of place here as Blair did.

"You ready?" Cal was as solicitous as a preppy waiter in one of Seattle's upscale restaurants. "Everything's good—and fresh too."

Blair ordered the potpie, wondering where Cal got his fresh groceries. Maybe that meant there was a good-sized town on down the road. She would see in the morning.

What she *really* craved was a martini. The kid at the counter was drinking a beer, and Blair didn't want to risk focusing on the men at the far table to see what they were having. They had to be the men from the silver truck; she had been unconsciously flirtatious with them, and she didn't want to send any more invitations. No more waving at truck drivers, she told herself.

One of them had put money in the jukebox. Tony Bennett's voice rose above the clatter in Cal's microcosm of a kitchen. Tony Bennett had been around so long, Blair thought, that she couldn't tell if it was a new record or one that had come with the jukebox.

She asked Cal about his beverage selections, and, wonder of wonders, he brought her back a really dry double martini. As she sipped it, she began to relax.

"You wanta dance?" The bigger of the two men was at her elbow; he had moved so quietly for someone his size.

Blair looked up at him, startled. He still wore sunglasses, although the sun had set an hour ago. He seemed clean enough in his white T-shirt and jeans; his blond hair was slicked back. He had a good cleft chin. Up close, he didn't seem so menacing—but she had learned her lesson. "Oh . . . n-no . . ." she stuttered. "I don't dance."

"Everybody dances." He smiled.

"I don't—really," she lied. "I had surgery . . . on my knee. A skiing accident."

"Yeah?"

"Yes, but thank you for asking."

"No problem."

She couldn't tell if he was disappointed, angry, or neutral. She thought he might ask the woman at the next table to dance, but he walked past without glancing at her.

Cal carried huge, bloody steaks to the truck drivers. They ate quickly, read the paper, lit cigarettes, and fed the jukebox. The teenager at the counter finished his food and left. Blair ate her meal, "read" her book, and tried not to look up.

She had noticed that there was a pay phone in the little entryway and thought about calling her mother. She decided against it; it was too public. Everyone in the place could hear her conversation. Somehow, she didn't want them to hear her name, or to know anything about her. There would be no messages on her answering machine, and that was good. She didn't want to hear Neil's "silence" on the tape. She had one blessing while she was gone. She was anonymous to him and everyone else.

The woman in the other booth stood beside her. Blair looked up and was surprised to see how tall she was—probably five-ten or so. She was perfectly groomed and carried a briefcase. Even close up, it was impossible to see her eyes.

"You staying over?" she asked Blair.

"Yes. The weather is terrible for driving at night."

"Me too." The woman's voice was soft and tentative. "There's something wrong with my car. I just don't know what I'm going to do. Aren't you frightened too?"

"Frightened? Why?" Blair asked.

"Oh . . ." The woman seemed vague, distracted. "Oh—of strangers. The news. Just things in the night—when you're alone. I was afraid when my car broke down . . . I had to leave it back on the road . . ."

Blair knew she should offer to help, but she had neither the energy nor the impulse to. "Maybe Cal can call someone for you in the morning."

"Maybe." The woman stood there like a wallflower at the prom. She smelled of cologne, a fragrance that Blair recognized but could not name. "I guess . . ."

Blair smiled awkwardly. "Good luck."

"Yes. Well . . . good night now. Lock up tight. Don't let the bedbugs bite."

Lord. Blair realized that warning might just be apropos at "-l's -abin K-mp." She pushed away most of the huge piece of apple pie that Cal had plopped down proudly; it tasted like artificial cinnamon and apple-flavored gum. *Fresh, my left foot.*

She wondered why she hadn't noticed a car broken down on the road. Maybe she had been too focused on avoiding the silver truck. It was only eight o'clock, but it felt to Blair as if it were midnight.

As she paid her check, she saw the headline of the *Wenatchee Daily World,* "Texas Serial Killer in Area." Perfect. That was all she needed. A serial killer. But they sure sold papers. Everybody was a serial killer. This week's serial killer was more dangerous than last week's. Despite herself, Blair lay a quarter and a dime next to the cash register and picked up a paper from the thin stack. If she couldn't get to sleep, she didn't want to be stuck with *Passages to Nowhere.*

As she started to open the door, the blond truck driver shouted, "You going so soon?"

"It's been a long day." She forced a careful smile.

"Stick around. We need to talk to you."

She shook her head. "I've got to be on the road early."

Why did she say that? Now, the men would know she was staying here. If she had just left, they might have assumed that she'd driven on. Her car was parked on the far side of her cabin.

"We don't bite," the man said, and walked a few steps toward her. "Promise. We're just damn sick of talking to each other. Have a cup of coffee with us—"

She looked at both men directly for the first time. They were younger than she had realized—probably not over twenty-five or so. Blair smiled a little more. "Rain check? Night now."

The blond man shrugged and turned toward the jukebox as Blair stepped out into the surprisingly chill air. Two headlights bounced toward her over the graveled area surrounded by whitewashed rocks. She saw that it was Cal driving an old Ford pickup. Where was *he* going?

"Sleep well, ma'am," he called from the cab.

"Don't you live here?" she asked.

"Nope—I've got a place a couple miles up the road. I'll just lock up the office and restaurant and I'll be on my way. Have a good night."

"You lock up the phone too?" she asked incredulously.

"Anyone wants me can call down to the house."

She didn't ask him what anyone who wanted to call out from his Kabin Kamp was supposed to do.

Blair could hear the truckers laughing and shouting at Cal as he drove away. They sounded a little drunk. She unlocked the door to Cabin #4, switched on the overhead light, and then immediately turned it off. She would have to pull the curtains or she would be on full display. Once she was certain there were no cracks between the dusty beige drapes, she turned the light back on.

The door's lock was flimsy and there was no chain. Blair propped a straight back chair under the knob, feeling paranoid—but not enough to forego this precaution. The windows were painted shut. There was a small window over the toilet in the cubicle Cal called a bathroom. Two lengths of rusty chain kept it from opening completely.

Blair decided to sleep in her clothes; it was cold enough to do that and not have to deride herself for being afraid. She picked up the newspaper and scanned the front page. " 'Vagabond Killer' spotted in Spokane. Gunnar Oscar Lundborg, 39, of Amarillo, Texas, is wanted for questioning in the strangulation deaths of nine professional women in five western states, and is thought to have been the man Spokane police stopped for questioning after a minor traffic collision yesterday. Lundborg, described as six feet tall and 175 pounds with blond hair and gray eyes, should be considered armed and dangerous . . ."

That description could fit a lot of men, she thought—even the big trucker in his blank, dark glasses.

Knowing full well that this was not what she should be reading if she had the faintest hope of getting a few hours sleep, Blair flipped anyway to the continuation of the coverage on Lundborg on page 8A. There was a mug shot, a blurred picture of what was purported to be the fugitive, dressed in a forest ranger's uniform, another wearing a security guard's uniform, and a montage of photographs of Lundborg's nine victims. They were all attractive white women—who appeared to be in their thirties or forties. Each of them smiled for some camera somewhere, unaware, Blair thought, that that particular picture would end up as it had—three columns wide in newspapers all over the country. What was the terrible synchronicity that had brought these women in contact with some violent, perhaps delusional, stranger to whom they would become no more than a notch on his belt? None of them had known each other. None of them had known Lundborg. Now they were bound together forever in some bleak sisterhood.

Lundborg was not a bad-looking man—for a serial killer. Blair felt a hysterical giggle in her throat. *Sure, Blair—As serial killers go, victims described him as quite attractive.*

Blair leapt from her bed, turned off the overhead light, and was back under the thin covers in one breath. It was completely dark. Cal had turned out even his mangled neon sign. The total blackness seemed almost palpable, as if it stroked her arms with velvet fingers and circled her head on the flat, hard pillow. All the events of her endless day came rushing back. She thought of the fog outside and tried to be grateful that it could not get in.

She wasn't sure if she had even been asleep when she heard the sound. Probably, she was in that fugue state between waking and sleeping. She had actually reached out her hand to turn off her alarm clock when she came fully awake and realized she wasn't home, that home was hundreds of miles away.

THE ROAD TRIP

The sound was soft—but insistent; Blair thought at first it was rain, but as she stared into blackness, she knew it wasn't. It was a scrabbling or a scratching along her door.

As she oriented herself to every corner of the cabin, trying to pinpoint the direction of the sounds, they grew louder. The scratching became steady knocking. Something hit the door. Had she not propped the chair there, it would surely have swung open. Blair lay, holding her breath, listening. After a spate of quiet, the scrabbling began again—this time at the window closest to her bed. Her teeth chattered as she slid out of bed to crouch behind it, away from the door.

Someone—or some *thing* was circling her cabin trying to get in. She heard the rattle of the short chains in the tiny bathroom window. And then it was at the door once more. The chair was, thank God, stronger than any of the other furniture. It held.

She couldn't see her watch, and she didn't dare turn on the light so she had no idea how long she knelt by her bed, listening. Silently, she picked up her purse and felt for the pepper spray canister. She held it, ready, in her hand.

After a long while, Blair's legs began to cramp and she needed to stretch out. But the floor was so creaky, she didn't dare to move.

"You in there?" a voice whispered. It was neither male nor female—nor human, for that matter.

"I *know* you're in there. Your car's still here."

She held her breath.

"Open the door. I just want to talk to you. Be a good girl."

She had never known how still she could be. Some instinct told her that even one word would be dangerous. Her breathing was so slow, she wondered how her heart could beat so fast.

After what seemed like hours, she heard the voice muttering—as if to someone else. "I don't think she's even in there."

She could not hear the answer. She waited.

And then she heard steps going away. She was not fooled; she did not crawl back into her bed. It had to be a trick. But whoever it was did not come back. Maybe he—*it?*—had been frightened away by something. Maybe it had been the truckers—drunk, loosed of all their inhibitions, who had come to their senses, finally, in the frigid air of early morning. Maybe. Not trusting, Blair waited, every muscle poised for flight, on the cold floor until she could see light at the bottom of the curtains.

She pulled back a curtain tentatively and felt its rotten cloth rip as she did, letting the sun stream in over the worn linoleum floor. She could see Cal's truck parked in front of the "Kafe." The long night might never have happened.

Blair wasn't going to wait around to see what Cal served for breakfast; she had her bags in her car in two minutes flat. As she slammed the trunk and turned toward the driver's door, she felt a soft touch on her arm.

"Please . . . can I go with you?"

It was the woman, her suit wrinkled, her makeup streaked. She looked exhausted—and terrified. "Someone was at my door in the night," she whispered. "I just know it was something awful—dangerous. Please take me with you. I can send a mechanic back . . ."

"Did you see who it was?" Blair asked. "Someone knocked on my door too . . ."

The woman seemed to be on the verge of tears. "No, I was afraid to look. I just want to get out of here. Let's go—*please,*" she begged, "He might still be around."

She gestured toward the rear of the restaurant, but Blair couldn't see anyone. She looked toward the shower shed. The silver truck was gone.

"Please? I'll get off at the next town."

"Sure," Blair said. "Get in." She *never* picked up hitchhikers, but she couldn't in good conscience leave the woman behind. She was probably as frightened as Blair was.

The fog was completely gone and the autumn colors were everywhere. Blair cracked her window; her passenger's cologne was overwhelming in the closed car—probably because Blair seldom wore perfume herself. She snuck peeks at the woman, who seemed quite calm now that they had left Cal's establishment and the night behind them.

"Do you live near here?" Blair asked.

"Not really." The woman's voice was even softer than she remembered it.

She tried again. "A long way from home?"

"You might say so."

Five minutes earlier, the woman had been half-sobbing; now her conversation was flat and somehow bitter. Blair felt the little hairs on her arms stand up. She stole a look at the woman's hands. Her nails were polished—a fashionable nutmeg color—but her hands were huge, and the bone at the joint of her hand and wrist bulged. Letting her eyes drop in her next surreptitious glance, Blair saw that her feet were slim but huge, and wondered where she had found pumps so large.

She didn't want to think what she was thinking.

"What's your first name?" Blair asked, trying to keep her voice steady. "If we're going to be riding together, I guess we should introduce ourselves."

"Gladys."

"I'm Blair . . ."

The woman sat awkwardly, her legs wide apart. Only the console of the Celica kept her left knee from touching Blair. Without really wanting to validate her suspicions, Blair pretended she needed to look to the right and back so she could move over from the passing lane. She looked at Gladys's neck. Above the large bow of her blouse, "Gladys" had an unmistakable Adam's apple.

Blair glanced down and saw with only faint surprise that "Gladys" also had a huge erection.

She cursed herself silently for being so stupid. But Blair knew how important it was that the man in drag believed he had fooled her. If she could somehow keep her voice steady and her fear hidden, maybe it would be all right. Maybe he was just some weird traveling salesman, with a kinky streak, who only wanted to be let off at the first gas station and garage.

Blair knew better. She knew who her passenger was—but she stalled for time. "Pretty morning, isn't it?"

"It's okay." He had dropped any pretense of disguising his voice. "We need to turn off up here—as soon as we find a sideroad."

Blair prayed to herself that there would be no side roads. Her own photograph, lined up with the first nine of Gunnar Lundborg's victims, kept playing through her mind.

"You know who I am, don't you?" he asked. "I saw you buy the paper."

"No . . . no," she lied. "I was so sleepy I didn't read the paper, Gladys."

"Gladys," he mimicked her. "Don't fuck with me."

She said nothing, but Blair pressed her foot down hard on the accelerator. If she went fast enough, he wouldn't have time to spot any hidden dirt roads leading off into some secret, silent place. She took the curves neatly, feeling her car's impulse to leave the road and correcting perfectly.

"Slow down," he ordered. But she ignored him. If she was going to die, it would be after a good fight. She went faster.

"Don't be stupid."

"I always drive this fast," she said tightly.

"You're gonna kill us both," he said, with just a trace of panic.

"Maybe. But that's the challenge of driving, isn't it? I would think you were up for living dangerously." She slid her eyes to the right for only an instant and saw that he was holding on to the door handle.

"I said, *Slow down!"*

She ignored him. As long as she was in the driver's seat, she had some control over whether she was going to live or die. Blair had no illusions that he would let her live once he got her away from the main road. As she rounded a tight curve to the left, she was sure they would sail off the road, but the Celica, weighted by her bags and sample cases in the hatchback, centered low and she was able to pull out of a spin.

"Look—you bitch," he said. "You do what I say—"

And then, miraculously, she saw the wide white apron and the gleaming gas pumps of a Texaco station far ahead. It had to be a mirage. Still, as they drew closer, she saw that it was real.

"I'm almost out of gas," she said. "I have to stop."

She hadn't seen the knife at all—but she felt it push through her sweatshirt into the skin of her right side, felt even the trickle of something wet sliding down her flesh. Oddly, she didn't feel pain. All of her other senses were completely aware—but she felt no pain.

Blair had no sense of being badly hurt; she felt neither faint not dizzy. He increased pressure on the knife as she pulled into the station. She wondered almost idly if he would actually kill her in front of someone. Inside her head, she marveled at how her mind was working when she felt utter, all-encompassing terror. She bypassed the Self-Service pumps and pulled to the Full-Serve. She needed to have the attendant come to her car window.

When Blair breathed in and out, the knife seemed to move with her. Her whole right side felt wet and she thought she could smell her own blood, a faint iodiny or metallic scent. But the man who walked lazily toward her wouldn't be able to see the scarlet stains on her sweatshirt. Gunnar Lundborg stared straight ahead, an expression of insane serenity on his face.

"Fill it up, please," Blair said. "And would you check under the hood?"

"Sure thing." The man wore greasy coveralls and moved so slowly that he might as well be underwater. He looked to be fifty or so, with a gut on him. He would be no match for Gunnar and his knife.

Blair felt Gunnar's eyes on her as she fished in her purse for her credit card. She handed it to the attendant, who barely glanced at her. When he presented the slip for her to sign, she willed him to look at her so that he would remember her. *Look at me. Look at me. . . .*

But he seemed totally oblivious to her and to her passenger. Blair turned slightly, pretending that she needed to steady the clipboard on her windowsill, and she raised the pen over the line for her signature, scribbling, "Call the police. I am being kidnapped. HELP!"

The gas station attendant met her eyes for an instant, muttered, "Thanks, and come again," and strolled off toward the office behind the glass windows.

"Drive," Gunnar snarled. "And keep it down."

"Where do you want me to go?" Blair asked. She was suddenly exhausted. The man at the gas station might look at that charge slip an hour from now, two days from now. It didn't matter; it would be too late. She could see the road ahead led into timberland. There was no town. She would soon be only a photograph to be released to the Associated Press.

"Now you'll do what I say, won't you?" Gunnar sounded arrogant, pleased with himself.

She nodded slightly. Her mind kept ducking into new corridors, trying to find a way out. She was surprised to find that she was angry. She had moved beyond fear, and she was enraged. "Take your knife out of my ribs."

"Why should I?"

"Because I'm driving and I'm beginning to feel like fainting, and if that happens, *you're* going to die."

To add emphasis to her warning, Blair drove faster. She knew now that was the one thing that frightened the maniac beside her. As far as she was concerned, she would rather die crashing head-on into a fir tree than as a result of what Gladys-Gunnar's fantasies dictated. She watched the speedometer climb with a kind of fatal fascination.

55 . . . 65 . . . 75 . . . The road beneath them had become a liquid ribbon. Blair sensed that her captor was reaching for the wheel, only to be thrown against the door as she took the curve. She took some pleasure in the curves that flung him heavily into the passenger door.

And then, the road straightened and Blair saw that it ended completely in a great silver rectangle with a jagged red streak across it. She experienced what it meant to stand on the brakes.

At that moment, the passenger door burst open and a tumble of blur of gray with a bright scarf flew out and smashed against a rock along the river. She expected him to leap to his feet, but he neither moved nor made a noise.

Blair felt as if she were still driving, but her car wasn't moving. She saw the sheriff's cars at each end of the truck, blocking the road completely. Someone was at her door and a strong arm wrenched it open and helped her out. She recognized the tattoos.

It was the blond truck driver. Without his dark glasses, she almost didn't know him. She would have asked him what he was doing there—but her knees had turned to Jell-O, and her voice seemed to be trapped way down inside of her.

"Lady, you are *stubborn,*" he said. "We tried to tell you last night that we smelled a rat—but you wouldn't even talk to us. We kept an eye on your cabin in the night, and we meant to convoy you this morning. We were turning the rig around and, when we got on the road, you were *gone.*"

"How did the sheriff get here?" Blair asked.

"You wrote a note at the gas station."

"But—he didn't even read it," she said incredulously. "He didn't even look at me—"

"Yes, he did. He was just smart enough not to let your friend there in the ditch know."

"Is he dead?" She looked back and saw that the gray rock was splashed with red.

"He's dead." The trucker led her to an aid unit that seemed to have magically appeared. He handed her up to the EMT as if she were as light as cotton candy, and she was grateful. She turned to thank him, and he grinned.

"Next time, remember—truck drivers may toot their horns at you, but we're a hell of a lot safer than serial killers. You're going to have to be more discriminating about who you trust. But, ma'am, you are one hell of a driver!"

"Thank you," Blair said carefully, her voice coming now from someplace at the end of a tunnel.

His words came from far away too. "We followed you across that mountain—it was late, and we knew you were going to hit the fog bank. I can't say we expected to meet *him*."

He banged the side of the medics' rig in a gesture that no longer seemed frightening, and then he was gone.

It was strange. When Blair went home to heal from the tic-tac-toe of knife wounds along her rib cage— shallow flesh wounds that were more bloody than serious—she discovered that she wasn't afraid any longer. She had come through the fire, and Neil's threats paled in comparison to what she had survived. She had been afraid of a dog, but she had beaten a tiger. When Neil phoned, she talked back to his silent breathing and he soon stopped phoning. When he drove by, she waved at him. When he left dead flowers on her front porch, she ordered even more desiccated blossoms delivered to his office. After a while, he went away.

The one thing that stayed with Blair was an eerie prickling sensation whenever the fog oozed in unbidden.

And that didn't happen very often.

Take It Away

Donald E. Westlake

N ice night for a stakeout."

Well, *that* startled me, let me tell you. I looked around and saw I was no longer the last person on line; behind me now was a goofy-looking grinning guy, more or less my age (34) and height (6'½"), but maybe just a bit thinner than my weight (190 lbs). He wore eyeglasses with thick black frames and a dark blue baseball cap turned around backward, with bunches of carroty red hair sticking out under it on the sides and back. He was bucktoothed and grinning, and he wore a gold and purple high school athletic jacket with the letter *X* hugely on it in Day-Glo white edged in purple and gold. It was open a bit at the top, to show a bright lime green polo shirt beneath. His trousers were plain black chinos, which made for a change, and on his feet were a pair of those high-tech sneakers complete with inserts and gores and extra straps and triangles of black leather here and there, that look as though they were constructed to specifications for NASA. In his left hand he held an *X-Men* comic book folded open to the middle of a story. He was not, in other words, anybody on the crew, or even *like* anybody on the crew. So what was this about a stakeout? Who *was* this guy?

Time to employ my interrogation techniques, which meant I should come at him indirectly, not asking *who are you* but saying, "What was that again?"

He blinked happily behind his big glasses and pointed with his free hand. "A stakeout," he said, cheerful as could be.

I looked where he pointed, at the side wall of this Burger Whopper where it was my turn tonight to get food for the crew, and I saw the poster there advertising this month's special in all twenty-seven hundred Burger Whoppers all across the United States and Canada, which was for their Special Thick Steak Whopper Sandwich, made with U.S. government–inspected steak guaranteed to be a full quarter-inch thick. I blinked at this poster, with its glossy color photo of the Special Thick Steak Whopper Sandwich, and beside me the goofy guy said, "A steak out, right? A great night to come out and get one of those steak sandwiches and bring it home and not worry about cooking or anything like that, because, who knows, the electricity could go off at any second."

Well, that was true. The weather had been miserable the last few days, hovering just around the freezing point, with rain at times and sleet at times and at the moment, nine-twenty P.M. on a Wednesday, outside the picture windows of the Burger Whopper, there crowded a thick misty fog, wet to the touch, kind of streaked and dirty, that looked mostly like an airport hotel's laundry on the rinse cycle.

Not a good night for a stakeout, not my kind of stakeout. All of the guys on the crew had been complaining and griping on our walkie-talkies, sitting in our cars on this endless surveillance, getting nowhere, expecting nothing, except maybe we'd all have the flu when this was finally over.

"See what I mean?" the goofy guy said, and grinned his bucktoothed grin at me again, and gestured at that poster like the magician's girl assistant gesturing at the elephant. See the elephant?

"Right," I said, and I felt a sudden quick surge of relief. If our operation had been compromised, after all this time and energy and effort, particularly given my own spotty record, I don't know what I would have done. But at least it wouldn't have been my fault.

Well, it hadn't happened, and I wouldn't have to worry about it. My smile was probably as broad and goofy as the other guy's when I said, "I see it, I see it. A steak out on a night like this, I get you."

"I'm living alone since my wife left me," he explained, probably feeling we were buddies since my smile was as moronic as his, "so mostly I just open a can of soup or something. But weather like this, living alone, the fog out there, everything so cold, you just kinda feel like you owe yourself a treat, you know what I mean?"

Mostly, I was just astonished that this guy had ever *had* a wife, though not surprised she'd left him. I've never been married myself, never been that fortunate, my life being pretty much tied up with the Bureau, but I could imagine what it must be like to have *been* married, and then she walks out, and now you're not married anymore. And what now? It would be like, if I screwed up *real* bad, much worse than usual, and the Bureau dropped me, and I wouldn't have the Bureau to go to anymore. I'd probably come out on foggy nights for a steak sandwich myself, and talk to strangers on the line at the Burger Whopper.

Not that I'm a total screwup, don't get me wrong. If I were a total screwup, the Bureau would have terminated me (not with prejudice, just the old pink slip) a long time ago; the Bureau doesn't suffer fools, gladly or otherwise. But it's true I have made a few errors along the way and had luck turn against me, and so on, which in fact was why I was on this stakeout detail in the first place.

All of us. The whole crew, the whole night shift, seven guys in seven cars blanketing three square blocks in the Meridian Hills section of Indianapolis. Or was it Ravenswood? How do I know, I don't know anything about Indianapolis. The Burger Whopper was a long drive away, that's all I know.

And we seven guys, we'd gotten this assignment, with no possibility of glory or advancement, with nothing but boredom and dyspepsia (the Burger Whopper is not my first choice of food) and chills and aches and no doubt the flu before it's over, because all seven of us had a few little dings and dents in our curricula vitae. Second-raters together, that's what we had to think about, losing self-esteem by the minute as we each sat alone there in our cars in the darkness, waiting in vain for Figuer to make his move.

Art smuggling; has there ever been a greater potential for boredom? Madonna and Child; Madonna and Child; Madonna and Child. Who cares what wall they hang on, as long as it isn't mine, those cow-faced Madonnas and fat-kneed Childs? Still, as it turns out, there's a lively illegal trade in stolen art from Europe, particularly from defenseless churches over there, and that means a whole lot of Madonnae und Kinder entering America rolled up in umbrellas or disguised as Genoa salami.

And at the center of this vast illegal conspiracy to bore Americans out of their pants was one Francois Figuer, a Parisian, now resident in the good old US of A. And he was who we were out to get.

We knew a fresh shipment of stolen art was on its way, this time from the defenseless churches of Italy and consisting mostly of the second favorite subject after M & C, being St. Sebastian, the bird condo. You know, the saint with all the arrows sticking out of him for the birds to perch on. Anyway, the Bureau had tracked the St. Sebastian shipment into the U.S., through the entry port at Norfolk, Virgina, but then had lost it. (Not us seven, some other bunch of screwups.) It was on its way to Figuer and whoever his customer might be, which is why we were here, blanketing his neighborhood, waiting for him to make his move. In the meantime, it was, as my new goofy friend had suggested, a good night for a steak out.

Seven men, in seven cars, trying to outwait and outwit one wily art smuggler. In each car, we had a police radio (in case we needed local backup), we had our walkie-talkie, and we had a manila folder on the passenger seat beside us, containing a map of the immediate area around Figuer's house and a blown-up surveillance photo of Figuer himself, with a verbal description on the back.

We sat in our cars, and we waited, and for five days nothing had happened. We knew Figuer was in the house, alone. We knew he and the courier must eventually make contact. We watched the arrivals of deliverymen from the supermarket and the liquor store and the Chinese restaurant, and when we checked, all three of them were the normal delivery- men from those establishments. Then we replaced them with our own deliverymen and learned only that Figuer was a lousy tipper.

Did he know he was being watched? No idea, but probably not. In any event, we were here, and there was no alternative. If the courier arrived, with a package that looked like a Genoa salami, we would pounce. If, instead, Figuer were to leave his house and go for a stroll or a drive, we would follow.

In the meantime, we waited, with nothing to do. Not allowed to read, even if we were permitted to turn on a light. We spoke together briefly on our walkie- talkies, that's all. And every night around nine, one of us would come here to the Burger Whopper to buy everyone's dinner. Tonight was my turn.

Apparently, everybody in the world felt thick fog created a good night to eat out, to counteract a foggy night's enforced slowness with some fast food. The line had been longer than usual at the Burger Whop- per when I arrived, and now it stretched another dozen people or so behind my new friend and me. A family of four (small, sticky-looking children, dazed father, furious mother), a young couple giggling and rubbing each other's bodies, another family, a hunched solitary fellow with his hands moving in his raincoat pockets, and now more beyond him.

Ahead, the end was in sight. Either the Whopper management hadn't expected such a crowd on such a night, or the fog had kept one or more employees from getting to work; whatever the cause, there was only one cash register in use, run by an irritable heavyset girl in the clownish garnet-and-gray Burger

Whopper costume. Each customer, upon reaching this girl, would sing out his or her order, and she would punch it into the register as though stabbing an enemy in his thousand eyes.

My new friend said, "It can get really boring sitting around in the car, can't it?"

I'd been miles away, in my own thoughts, brooding about this miserable assignment and the miserable weather, and without thinking I answered, "Yeah, it sure can," but then immediately caught myself and stared at the goof again and said, *"What?"*

"Boring sitting around in the car," he repeated. "And you get all stiff after a while."

This was true, but how did *he* know? Thinking, What is going *on* here? I said, "What do you mean, sitting around in the car? What do you mean?" And at the same time now thinking, Can I take him into protective custody?

But the goof spread his hands, gesturing at the Burger Whopper all around us, and said, "That's why we're here, right? Instead of over at Radio Special."

Well, yes. Yes, that was true. Radio Special, another fast-food chain with a franchise joint not far from here, was set up like the drive-in deposit window at the bank. You drove up to the window, called your order into a microphone, and a staticky voice told you how much it would cost. You put the money into a bin that slid out and back in, and a little later the bin would slid out a second time, with your food and your change. A lot of people prefer that sort of thing, because they feel more secure being inside their own automobiles, but us guys on stakeout find it too much of the same old same old. What we want, when there's any kind of excuse for it, is to be *out* of the car.

So I had to agree with my carrot-topped friend. "That's why I'm here, all right. I don't like sitting around in a car any more than I have to."

"I'd hate a *job* like that, I can tell you," he said.

There was no way to respond to that without blowing my cover, so I just smiled at him and faced front.

The person next ahead of me on line was being no trouble at all, for which I was thankful. Slender and attractive, with long, straight, ash blond hair, she was apparently a college student, and had brought along a skinny green looseleaf binder full of her notes from some sort of math class. Trying to read over her shoulder, I saw nothing I recognized at all. But then she became aware of me and gave a disgusted little growl, and hunched further over her binder, as though to hide her notes from the eavesdropper. Except that I realized she must have thought I was trying to look down the front of her sweater—it would have been worth the effort, but in fact I hadn't been—and I got suddenly so embarrassed I automatically took a quick step backward and tromped down on the goof's right foot.

"Ouch!" he said, and gave me a little push, and I got my feet back where they belonged. "Sorry," I said. "I just—I don't know what happened."

"You violated my civil rights there," he told me, "that's what happened." But he said it with his usual toothy grin.

What *was* this? For once, I decided to confront the weirdness head-on. "Guess it's a good thing I'm not a cop, then," I told him, "so I *can't* violate your civil rights."

"To tell you the truth," he said, "I've been wondering what you do for a living. I know it's nosy of me, but I can't ever help trying to figure people out. I'm Jim Henderson, by the way, I'm a high school math teacher."

He didn't offer to shake hands, and neither did I, because I was mostly trying to find an alternate occupation for myself. I decided to borrow my sister's husband. "Fred Barnes," I lied. "I'm a bus driver, I just got off my tour."

"Ah," he said. "I've been scoring math tests, wanted to get away from it for a while."

Mathematicians in front of me and behind me; another coincidence. It's all coincidence, nothing to worry about.

"I teach," Jim Henderson went on, "up at St. Sebastian's."

I stared at him. "St. Sebastian's?"

"Sure. You know it, don't you? Up on Rome Road."

"Oh, sure," I said.

The furious mother behind us said, "Move the line up, will ya?"

"Oh," I said, and looked around, and my girl math student had moved forward and was now second in line behind the person giving an order. So I was third, and the goof was fourth, and I didn't have much time to think about this.

Was something up, or not? If I made a move, and Jim Henderson was merely Jim Henderson just like he'd said, I could be in big trouble, and the whole stakeout operation would definitely be compromised. But if I *didn't* make a move, and Jim Henderson actually turned out to be the courier, or somebody else connected with Francois Figuer, and I let him slip through my fingers, I could be in big trouble all over again.

I realized now that it had never occurred to any of

us that anybody else might listen in on our walkie-talkie conversations, even though we all knew they weren't secure. From time to time, on the walkie-talkies, we'd heard construction crews, a street-paving crew, even a movie crew on location, as they passed through our territory, talking to one another, but the idea that Francois Figuer, inside his house, might have his own walkie-talkie, or even a scanner, and might listen to us, had never crossed our minds. Not that we talked much, on duty, back and forth, except to complain about the assignment or arrange our evening meal—

Our evening meal.

Who was Jim Henderson, what was he? I wished now I'd studied the picture of Francois Figuer more closely, but it had always been nighttime in that damn car. I'd never even read the material on the back of the picture. Who was Francois Figuer? Was he the kind of guy who would do . . . whatever this was?

Was all this—please God—after all, just coincidence?

The customer at the counter got his sack of stuff and left. The math girl stood before the irritable Whopper girl and murmured her order, her voice too soft for me to hear; on purpose, I think. She didn't want to share *anything,* that girl.

I didn't have much more time to think, to plan, to decide. Soon it would be my turn at the counter. What did I have to base a suspicion on? Coincidence, that's all. Odd phrases, nothing more. If coincidences didn't happen, we wouldn't need a word for them.

All right. I'm ahead of Jim Henderson, I'll place my order, I'll get my food, I'll go outside, I'll wait in the car. When he comes out, I'll follow him. We'll see for sure who he is and where he goes.

254

Relieved, I was smiling when the math girl turned with her sack. She saw me, saw my smile, and gave me a contemptuous glare. But her good opinion was not as important as my knowing I now had a plan, I could now become easier in my mind.

I stepped up to the counter, fishing the list out of my pants pocket. Seven guys, and every one of us wanted something different. I announced it all, while the irritable girl spiked the register as though wishing it were *my* eyes, and throughout the process I kept thinking.

Where did Jim Henderson live? Could I find out by subtle interrogation techniques? Well, I would say, we're almost done here. Got far to go?

I turned. "Well," I said, and watched the mother whack one of her children across the top of the head, possibly in an effort to make him as stupid as she was. I saw this action very clearly because there was no one else in the way.

Henderson! Whoever! Where *was* he? All this time on line, and just when he's about to reach the counter he *leaves?*

"The man!" I spluttered at the furious mother and pointed this way and that way, more or less at random. "He—Where—He—"

The whole family gave me a look of utter unalterable treelike incomprehension. They were going to be no help at all.

Oh, hell, oh, damn, oh, gol*darn* it! Henderson, my eye! He's, he's, he's either Figuer himself or somebody connected to him, and I let the damn man escape!

"Wenny sen fory three."

I started around the family, toward the distant door. The line of waiting people extended almost all the way down to the exit. Henderson was nowhere in sight.

"Hey!"

"Hey!"

The first hey was from the irritable Whopper girl, who'd also been the one who'd said wenny sen foyr three, and the second hey was from the furious mother. Neither of them wanted me to complicate the routine.

"You gah *pay* futhis!"

Oh, God, oh, God. Time is fleeting. Where's he gotten to? I grabbed at my hip pocket for my wallet, and it wasn't there.

He picked my pocket. Probably when I stepped on his foot. Son of a *bitch!* Money. ID.

"Cancel the order!" I cried, and ran for the door.

Many people behind me shouted that I couldn't do what I was already doing. I ignored them, pelted out of the Whopper, ran through the thick gray swirling fog toward my car, my face and hands already clammy when I got there, and unlocked my way in.

Local police backup, that's what I needed. I slid behind the wheel, reached for the police radio microphone, and it wasn't there. I scraped knuckles on the housing, expecting the microphone to be there, and it wasn't there.

I switched on the interior light. The curly black cord from the mike to the radio was cut and dangling. He'd been in the car. *Damn* him. I slapped open the manila folder on the passenger seat and wasn't at all surprised that the photo of Francois Figuer was gone.

Would my walkie-talkie reach from here to the neighborhood of the stakeout? I had no idea, but it was my last means of communication, so I grabbed it up from its leather holster dangling from the dashboard—at least he hadn't taken *that*—thumbed the side down, and said, "Tome here. Do you read me? Calling anybody. Tome here."

And then I noticed, when I thumbed the side down to broadcast, the little red light didn't come on.

Oh, that bastard. Oh, that French . . .

I slid open the panel on the back of the walkie-talkie, and of course the battery pack that was supposed to be in there was gone. But the space wasn't empty, oh, no. A piece of paper was crumpled up inside there, where the battery used to be.

I took the paper out of the walkie-talkie and smoothed it on the passenger seat beside me, and it was the Figuer photo. I gazed at it. Without the thick black eyeglasses, without the buck teeth, without the carroty hair sticking out all around from under the turned-around baseball cap, this was him. It was *him*.

I turned the paper over, and now I read the back, and the words popped out at me like neon: "reckless" "daring" "fluent unaccented American English" "strange sense of humor."

And across the bottom, in block letters in blue ink, had very recently been written: "They forgot to mention master of disguise. Enjoy your steak out. FF"